Mating Scars

A novella by

Scott L. Miller

ISBN

Hardcover:978-1-966565-48-2

Paperback:978-1-966565-49-9

Other Novels by Scott L. Miller

Interrogation (first in the Mitchell Adams series)

Counterfeit (second in the Mitchell Adams series)

The Virtual Suicide Machine (third in the Mitchell Adams series)

Boundless (fourth in the Mitchell Adams series)

Prodigal

The Nostradamus Society

To those who don't fit in the regular nine-to-five world.

"The secret of being a top-notch con man is being able to know what the mark wants, and how to make him think he's getting it."

Ken Kesey

"I've always loved movies about con men. I think con men are as American as apple pie."

Bill Paxton

"Even a good player will someday become a toy of a better player. It's called Karma."

Unknown origin

Contents

The House Always Wins

"There is no greater rush than watching the hunter become the hunted."

Lola

She initiates the ritual dance across the smoke-filled bar simply when she enters the room. The female capuchin monkey often must whine, pout, shake bushes, and even throw stones at a male to attract his attention. The version of Hominidae that mistakenly rules the planet for the time being is far easier. All she did to set her plan in motion was make eye contact with him and offer the faintest of smiles. She'd already chosen him, and the silly monkey didn't know it yet. She orders a Grey Goose martini and takes a healthy pull. Ten minutes later, the bartender places a second drink in front of her.

"From the gentleman in the bomber jacket at the other end of the bar," the bartender says with a wink as he takes her empty glass and wipes the dark mahogany counter.

"Thanks, Rob."

A customer standing behind her calls out drink orders over the jukebox din of a Thorogood song that talks about 'one bourbon, one scotch, and one beer.' Off goes Rob with the towel slung over a hefty shoulder once he exchanges her full ashtray for a clean one.

She guesses three seconds. She raises her glass and broadens her smile at the bomber jacket. Sure enough, three seconds later, the monkey rises from his barstool. Her suspicion about the watch as he approaches is spot on. Her other assumption about him also brings a smile to her face:

the gold wedding band on his ring finger. He's shorter than she expects, at least a good four inches shorter than her, but who can tell someone's height when they're sitting across from you in a darkened bar? Besides, height is irrelevant for this.

The bar stools on both sides of hers are occupied, so when he walks up to her left, she leans toward him, holding an unlit cigarette in one hand. He places his half-empty Budweiser on the bar and extracts a gold lighter from his pocket. She cups a hand over his and meets his dark brown eyes as she sucks on the filter until the tip grows orange. His hairy, black tufts spill out from the front of his denim shirt and over a gold chain; even the skin between his knuckles is furry. His canned tan doesn't quite reach his lower eyelids.

Definitely a monkey.

She blows smoke up and above his face. "Thanks. For the light and the drink."

The couple to her right gets up to leave, and he moves quickly to grab the seat next to her before another couple can sit. He makes a point of running his fingers across her shoulder and the nape of her neck while he circles behind her, assessing for discomfort or resistance. He feels none.

"Looks like this is my lucky day, little lady." While he takes the chair next to her, he doesn't notice her suppress a smile over his choice of words.

He moves the stool closer to hers. "Looked like you needed a refill and some company. That's a nice dress, very flattering." He reaches across her to grab his beer. "I'm George. The dealers here call me Mr. G. What's your name, darling?"

The dress is a Goodwill special from last year. Leopard print, form-fitting, with a plunging neckline the way she chooses to wear it. It reveals the top of a bumblebee tattoo near her heart. "Lola. You gamble here often?" She toys with the olive between her lips before she swallows. He grins as he watches every movement her mouth makes, probably assigning meaning to the casual act.

She senses his chest swell as he nods. "Most weekend nights, you can find me in the poker room. No limit. And most nights, like tonight, I drive them from the table, cursing straight to the ATM. You a gambler, darling?"

She shakes her head and laughs. "God, no. I work too hard for my money to risk losing it." She makes a show of fumbling for the keys in her purse as her skirt rides up a few extra inches, then takes a healthy swig and places her hand on his shoulder as she turns to him. "So, you think you're good at reading people. What kind of person am I, Mr. G? What do I do for a living?"

He drains his beer and casually settles a hand on her knee while he studies her face. He reserves his first thought for himself. "You're a woman who likes to party after a hard day's work. You work with people. In the service industry. No, I would say you're a ... model." He shoots a furtive glance at the bar and snaps his fingers. "I got it! You're a stewardess on layover."

Men on the hunt often say they think she's a model and then say: *well, if you aren't, you should be.* It's their lame opening gambit to flatter and coax, like the female capuchin monkey. She doesn't consider herself all that attractive, though she does like her long brown hair that hangs below her ass. In fact, the only attribute that qualifies her to be a model is her height. She flashes a look of genuine surprise and excitement, even though she placed her car keys and Southwest Airlines keychain in plain sight next to her purse. "That's incredible! How could you possibly know I'm a stew?" She echoes his obsolete term while she realizes this curious little George looks much older up close.

His hand moves up from her knee to her thigh and meets no resistance. He positions his face so close to her ear that she smells faint cigar breath. "That's why I'm a winner, darling. I have a sixth sense. I know who I'm up against."

She drains her glass and touches his arm again, thinking *that's hilarious*. "I think I'm a bit tipsy, Mr. No Limits."

His beer breath fills her ear. "I have a suite on the top floor. There's a Ja-cuz (he emphasizes the second syllable … gross), wet bar, maybe some party favors if you're game."

His mention of *game* causes her smile to return. "Then what are we doing here, George?"

He slaps a twenty on the counter, wraps an arm around her waist, and they exit the dark, noisy bar. The bright lights on the casino floor force her to squint, and she feels a brief, stabbing pain above and behind her right eye that momentarily staggers her. Her vision blurs for the second time tonight as they stroll through the casino. A cacophony of jingly-jangly music, the whir of spinning wheels, loud beeps, and chimes from ubiquitous slot machines almost drown out the chatter of determined gamblers while big screens high on the walls broadcast a football game from a snowy field. Now she sees the bald spot on his head and the bags under his eyes. This horny little monkey must be in his late fifties. He reminds her of her old man, which makes it better.

He regards the people slouched or huddled over colorful rows of flashing slots with amusement. "Look at these suckers. There's a reason they call 'em one-armed bandits. The law of diminishing returns hooks them. One small payout excites them, so they eagerly throw good money after bad while they wait, and wait, and wait for the bigger one that never comes. That's why I play people. Let me tell you, darling, the young poker studs think they're hot shit players until they sit down at my table. They never know what hit 'em. Know what I mean?" He squeezes her tighter.

Her vision clears. *I feel the same way. We're a lot alike.* "Wow, that last martini really hit me." She makes a show of being unsteady on her feet, and his hand lingers on her breast as he supports her down the hallway to the elevators.

They walk past the check-in desk, and she averts her face from the concierges as they check in late-Friday night arrivals. It turns out his room isn't on the top floor, it's not a suite, and she learns later that it doesn't even have a *Ja-cuz*, but she keeps it to herself while he places the Do-Not-Disturb sign outside the door and rattles home the cheap safety chain.

He kisses her hard and slides a hand between her legs before she can remove her coat. Behind him, she notices a battered cardboard case of various cheap wines and house liquor bottles on the coffee table. The so-called wet bar.

"I have an idea. Why don't you call your stew friends and see if they're up for a party? Y'all staying at the hotel on a layover, right?"

She steps back and pulls out her phone. "Sure. Let me take my coat off, and I'll call Gretchen and Kim. They're twins. They're a little younger but love to party." She touches his chest, and her eyes widen as she whispers into his ear. "And we really, really appreciate party favors. Be a doll and point me to the restroom." She dials a number on speed dial as he does so.

"This is room 908, right?"

He mumbles a breathy *hell yes* and starts to unzip her dress, but she makes for the hallway before he can finish. "Why don't you make me a drink and bring out the party favors while I talk to the girls?"

From behind, she hears him pull off his cowboy boots and remove his jacket. He whistles a gleeful country tune off-key.

Caked beard stubble stains the tiny sink, and wet towels line the floor in front of the shower tub. A faint smell of mildew assaults her nose, and she grimaces. She locks the door, runs water in the sink, and turns on the vent fan before she opens the medicine cabinet.

He creeps to the bathroom door in his shorts and puts his ear next to it. He tries to remember what he has in there and decides it's safe—just Viagra, Rogaine, some prescription meds with zero street value, and a safety razor. Lola hasn't asked him for money yet, but his first thought was that she's a hooker, and he knows better than to let strange women or hookers out of his sight for long. Through the door, he hears: "Hey, Gretch, it's me. If you and Kim don't already have plans, you're invited to a party. No? Great! He's cute and can hook us up." A pause, followed by the whir of toilet paper, then: "Great, see you then. We're in room 908." When the toilet flushes, he hustles back to the bedroom to make the drinks.

He hands her a bathroom glass with vodka on the rocks. "Your friends gonna make this a group party?"

She smiles at the two lines on the glass tray. "In about an hour, but I can't wait that long." She steps out of her dress and reveals a matching red lace bra and panties.

He makes for the bathroom. "Hold that thought, darling. Be right back."

She smiles and bends over the lines. *He's rushing for the Viagra, no doubt,* as she wipes her nose clean and runs her fingertips along her gums. She takes a pill from her purse, finds his drink, and places her phone on silent mode. She stirs his drink.

She carries their drinks to the bedroom and offers a toast after the monkey snorts his line and climbs into bed. "To all the young players, Mr. G fleeced tonight! May they all return to his table!" Whether it's the coke or the adrenaline rush from her ritual, the air feels charged with electricity, the act of breathing becomes a torrid proposition, and her heart races. The uncertainty of the outcome excites her. The success or failure of the hunt makes her feel alive. She offers a second toast and delays his advances long enough for him to down most of his drink; then, when she can no longer stall, he climbs on top of her. He kisses with his eyes closed the entire time, something she never does. His lips move to her bumblebee tat and breasts while she unrolls a condom on the nightstand for him. When he climaxes, she bites his shoulder and draws blood. He protests, but she quickens her hip movements until he hardens and comes again, this time so weak she barely feels it. He turns toward her and drifts off to sleep on his side, the silverback offering his throat to the lioness. *And he wanted two extra girls!* She stares at the black-gray hairs that sprout from his ears and nostrils while he snores. Up close, he resembles her father in some ways— broad nose, thick neck, '70s porn-star mustache, and gold chain necklace. Who wears those anymore? The more similarities she finds, the more she wants to hurt this monkey, but she sticks to the plan. She waits thirty more minutes until the clock on the opposite wall reaches three a.m. The pill did its job.

Sex, the ultimate charade of safety.

She tiptoes to the drawers (nothing but clothes here), then the closet (only an empty piece of luggage there), then quietly looks under the bed and pulls out a men's tack and garment bag. The snoring continues uninterrupted as she carefully squats at the foot of the bed and slowly goes through the pockets. She reads papers that indicate he owns a home remodeling company. She takes fifteen large, a vial of coke, and a loaded .38 before she carefully returns the bag under the bed. She dresses and helps herself to the cash from his wallet, his driver's license and the photo of his pudgy wife and two pudgy kids. She pockets his phone and the platinum Rolex. She slowly removes the gold chain from his neck, which causes him to snore and roll to his other side. She hides his car keys behind the television. To be safe, she wipes her glass and the surfaces she touched in the bathroom. The snoring on the bed holds steady as she silently closes the door behind her. She puts on her stilettoes in the empty, garishly colored hallway.

So many details go unnoticed in the big, bad world, and Mr. G., a self-anointed reader and fleecer of unsuspecting gamblers, will wake up with a headache to find himself thoroughly schooled.

She buys a large, floppy hat at an over-priced gift shop, saunters through the parking garage to bypass the concierge desk, and takes the steps to a distant open-air lot where she had earlier parked her old white SUV, away from the security cameras. The drive home takes ninety minutes; the smart hunter never hunts close to home. The first thing she does at home is let Jack out. She stands hugging herself against the cold in the small backyard while she waits for the pit bull to do his business. She enters the monkey's address in her phone before she sets the driver's license afire with her lighter. His photo blackens and curls into an amorphous blob. She places the family picture atop it. She took both to send a message that she knew where they lived and not to look for her. Worst case scenario, he could sober up in twelve hours and demand photos of her from casino security, but she doubts he'll do that. She smiles at the image of the little chimp chattering away to the hotel manager, perhaps jumping up and down in righteous anger, swinging his hirsute arms, and demanding personal information for a group of non-existent stewardesses, especially Lola and twins named Gretchen and Kim (the number she dialed from Mr. G's hotel bathroom was the local time and temperature). She earned enough tonight to pay two months' mortgage and car payments. She stashes the watch and chain (with others and a stack of bills) under a loose floorboard to pawn months later in another state. She feeds Jack and takes a shower as dawn breaks. She swallows Xanax from a prior spoil of war to counteract her coke high and climbs into bed, but sleep is interrupted by the black silhouette of a man from her stolen childhood that returns to haunt her.

If she'd looked out her window before she climbed into bed, she would have noticed a nondescript Camry parked across the street. The powerfully built, long-haired man in the driver's seat followed her home from the casino. He climbed her wooden fence to peer into the backyard, but Jack had run to the fence barking and growling, which drove the man back to his car.

Achilles' Heel

"Even the queen of the jungle dies. I want it to be on my terms."

Alicia

The white SUV rattles to a stop in one of the many hospital parking garages in this monstrosity of a complex. Alicia rides an elevator to the basement floor that houses the MRI machines. The unit secretary behind the glass requests to see her Medicare and Medicaid cards to ensure they are transferred into the hospital's new software program. Dressed in a plain black sweater and jeans, she sits in a crowded waiting room thirty minutes past her scheduled appointment. The room is filled mostly with elderly patients. She flips through year-old magazines and surfs the internet. As each minute passes, she does a slow burn because these invariably turn out to be all-day affairs, counting the hour drive each way. She hates every sad sight, each antiseptic smell, and whiny sound that regularly occurs in hospitals; the sick and the weak flock here to die like lemmings after the system strips their every dollar and thread of dignity. She promises that will not happen to her.

She sighs in relief when Barb finally appears to escort her down the hall, upbeat and always smiling for the patients and families. She's short, overweight, sixtyish, a bottled blonde in a pixie cut, trying too hard to be young again. To her, she's a peacock, with her bright, red-framed glasses that seem to fill her entire round face, her fire engine red lipstick and nails, the garish colored scrubs she chooses to wear, and the gaudy wedding ring and earrings.

From other visits, she knows Barb devotes special attention and care to people like her, those with illnesses that could snuff out their young lives in minutes. "You look so pretty today! I love your hair. I used to wear mine not quite as long as yours, but the older I get short hair becomes a time saver, what with everything else going on in my life."

Barb notes her vitals and asks if she's experiencing any persistent headaches, vision changes, nausea or vomiting, light sensitivity, neck stiffness or pain, facial numbness, and pain above or behind the eyes since her last visit. Alicia denies them all. Barb glances at the chart. "Let's see, your last reading was 2.6." She moves closer, to manipulate her neck and complete her standard visual assessment while she chatters on about her life. Then Alicia changes into scrubs in a nearby cubicle, grateful to tune out the drivel when Barb can't see her. She rolls her eyes and yawns while Barb prattles on about the upcoming holidays, her sons' problems, her inattentive husband, and she even resurrects some droll minutiae from twenty years ago about her ex-husband. She takes comfort that Barb knows nothing about her life other than what little the sterile medical chart contains. Whenever Barb presses her to share parts of herself, she invents positive spin stories designed to make her appear self-sufficient, kind, and socially aware, which is fun and causes her to smile. The only downside is it forces her to remember each lie. Today, she longs to be trapped inside the cramped MRI cylinder, with orange-colored earplugs that only partially muffle the hundred-decibel thumping of the metal coils in the machine as they vibrate and bang together, all while she fights the severe claustrophobic feeling that rises inside her. Closing her eyes and meditating helps some, but the time still passes too slowly. In past times, she would press the panic button to stop the machine when she wanted to move or felt like she needed attention or sympathy.

Alicia has been coming here for eight years, and Barb has been her clinic nurse the last year. She places her car keys, purse, and shoes in a plastic tray and secures it all in a small bank of lockers.

The moment she flings open the curtain, Barb walks up to her, invading her personal space. She notices part of the bumblebee tattoo that protrudes from the scrub top. "I love that little bee, but it doesn't seem to suit you because you're so sweet."

"Bees may sting, but they also play a key role in making honey. I know you told me you have a tat. I forget, is it a peacock?"

Barb pats her ample right buttock. "It's a butterfly. So, what do you think?"

She chides herself for not paying more attention. "The butterfly?"

Barb touches her shoulder. "No. About Christmas, silly. Staying at our house for a few days. I know you're not close to your mother, and this time of year can be depressing, at least it is for me. You've said you're not much of a cook, but I'm a very good one."

Her eyebrows raise. Is Barb a lonely, lost peacock looking for something that's missing in her life? If so, what is it? At a loss for words, she hangs the locker key by the treatment room door. "I'm sorry, I didn't hear the invite from the changing room."

Barb reaches out to touch her arm. "Well, what do you say?"

Most of her wants to politely and immediately decline, but the bizarreness of it intrigues her. "I can't make any promises. Let me talk to my mom first about when she's having Christmas, but yes, that's very kind of you. Thanks."

"Great! We can work around your schedule. Gary won't care. He does his own damn thing most of the time anyway."

The inattentive pharmacist husband who makes her a golf widow nine months out of the year. Last summer, Barb mentioned they own a house in the suburbs that she personally decorated and designed to transform it into a home. It sounds big and fancy, with two good incomes.

She *is* a peacock. One who seems to be looking to regain her strut on some level.

Alicia negotiates the time trapped in the MRI tube without incident this afternoon.

While she changes back into her street clothes, Barb regurgitates the usual post-test speech like a good little nurse. "Dr. Chen will call you with the results. Let's hope it stays at 2.6. It's good you're not having symptoms."

If you only knew, Alicia thinks while she smiles. The ill-advised drinking and drug use, the light sensitivity, blurred vision, and headaches.

"In the meantime, avoid alcohol and eat the healthy diet the dietician recommended. Exercise daily to get that heart rate up, but don't overdo it."

When she pulls back the privacy curtain, Barb is two feet away and hands her two cards, one at a time. "Here's your next scheduled appointment with Dr. Chen. Monday, three months from now at the same time, like you requested. The next visit is just an exam and lab work, no machine. We will mail the orders for your next lab draw when the time nears. Sorry, Doc was called away today. My cell is on the back of the second card. Call me when you know your plans with your mom. This is going to be fun!"

She pastes a smile on her face long enough to say, "I look forward to it."

"You're so dedicated, with your church involvement helping the elderly and volunteering at the local food bank two days a week, all while you rehab your house. Gary can barely change a lightbulb without making a Broadway production out of it or alerting the media. You're so young; don't forget to make time for a social life, too."

Alicia smiles again, feeling almost sorry for the poor nudnik. The house rehab part is the only true part. "I enjoy helping others. I do what I can to help."

Barb escorts her down the aisle to the main hallway and places a hand on her shoulder. "You're in my prayers. Be safe driving home, and call me."

Her SUV will not start. She uses the red emergency phone in the parking garage to summon security. An older man with a pot belly arrives in fifteen minutes, gives her a jump, and suggests she have her mechanic check the remaining shelf life of her battery, as this is the second time he's had to do this.

She hits the drive-through for a sack of White Castle belly bombers (not on her diet) and a Coke for the ride home, even though it means she'll face rush-hour traffic leaving the city.

The more she thinks about this afternoon, the more she wonders if she unconsciously planted the seeds of this invitation months ago, given her fictional hospital persona. To her shock, it spurred the MRI staff to adopt her as an indigent patient last Christmas; she received cash, gift certificates, gas cards, clothes, and a good winter coat. If she did half-knowingly cast her net upon these bountiful waters, Barb seems more than willing to offer more bait.

She imagines that the idea of a married RN who invites a sick clinic patient on disability to sleepover as a guest in her home for days must run counter to some hospital rule, cross some caregiver/patient boundary, or at the very least display a significant lapse in judgment. Barb may be nothing more than a lonely older woman choosing her as the object of her good Catholic deed for Christmas, or this may be a way to make herself feel good instead of feeling depressed over the holidays, but she doubts it. Hearing her drone on about her ungrateful adult children and how badly they treat her suddenly makes Alicia want to learn more about Barb and the inattentive pharmacist husband. They do have money.

If her read is right, Barb is a fellow lost soul, but of a different nature. There are two kinds of people in this world: the heartbroken and the heartbreakers. Heartbroken, Barb forever searches for someone to fill her broken cup, but the break in her cup is too damn wide and can never be filled. She's a perpetual victim, but for some reason, this smart person has yet to realize this during her sixty-some-odd years. Alicia smiles at the truth that people possess several types of intelligence. If so, this non-street-wise peacock can be used to her advantage.

Could a big-risk, big-reward long game be in the works? This one involves two intelligent, well-to-do, professional people and possibly their adult children. More moving parts means more things could go south along the way.

❀ ❀ ❀

As she crosses the Poplar Street Bridge into Illinois, she reflects on her last long game that involved only two people who weren't nearly as intellectually smart as Barb and her pharmacist husband.

Last year, an acquaintance named 'Savannah' befriended a reclusive old lady through her church and overheard the tail end of a brief but volatile argument the old woman had on the church steps with her only child. She told him she'd rather leave everything to her cats than to an ungrateful son who was too busy to make time for her. Savannah offered to help Myrtle, so she became a friendly ear and, over the next months, gradually inserted herself into Myrtle's life—after-church chats over tea turned into filling her weekly pill reminder box, shopping and meal preparation, cleaning those disgusting cat litter boxes, and other light housework in exchange for a paltry hourly wage. A child of the Great Depression, Myrtle believed wages (but not prices) had stagnated since the '50s. Savannah happened to be returning from the grocery store the day the police found Myrtle wandering outside barefoot in her nightgown. The officer wanted to call her son, but Savannah told the cop that she was Myrtle's duly appointed caretaker and that she would make the call. Once the cop left, Myrtle begged her not to contact her son, certain "he'll put me in a nursing home." In exchange for not calling the son, she convinced Myrtle that she had to hire more help to keep her out of a nursing home, which terrified the old gal more than death itself. Savannah maneuvered her into hiring her friend Alicia for the nighttime shift. Alicia played her role to perfection, but Myrtle insisted her starting wage had to be less than Savannah's until she gained the old gal's trust. Alicia thought the old bag of bones reminded her of a turtle, wrinkled and slow and a prisoner in her decaying little shell. During the first two months of a night shift, Alicia snuck men into the home while the turtle slept and, like Savannah, grew adept at picking the right occasions to pocket small amounts of cash here and there, but not enough in their minds to make up for the paltry wages. This was no easy task, for the turtle was paranoid about her money and possessions and even pencil-marked her liquor bottles. Near the end of winter, late fees and unpaid bills began to arrive, and Myrtle complained to Savannah about them. She could no longer properly manage her checkbook and didn't trust electronic or automatic payments, so she wrote every check by hand and sent it via snail mail. The penny pincher complained to the heavens about the fee her bank wanted to charge for the service. Savannah offered to do it for free, but they'd have to drive to the bank and place her name on the turtle's checks. Savannah unplugged the trickle charger from the turtle's massive old Cadillac and backed it out. The sixteen-year-old tank of an auto had 12,000 miles on it, and were it not for the trickle charger that her ungrateful son had installed in the garage, the car battery would be as dead as Julius Caesar. Savannah decided that she alone should accompany the turtle to her bank. One younger, unknown person showing up with Myrtle would draw less suspicion than two, especially since the turtle trusted Savannah because of their church affiliation.

As rehearsed, Myrtle did the talking. Once Savannah helped settle her with the portable oxygen tank into the chair, Myrtle introduced Mrs. Forni, the bank manager, to Savannah as her caregiver from church.

The rest of the conversation between the two was relayed later by Savannah and remains a bone of contention by Alicia.

"I want to add my caregiver's name to my account so she can pay my bills." Her gnarled fingers grip the blue checkbook cover tightly, her skin nearly translucent and pockmarked by age spots.

"Oh," Mrs. Forni says, slightly taken aback. "We discussed this on the phone some time ago. The bank can provide the service safely for a modest fee—"

Myrtle chuckled and rolled her eyes. She was far too old to stuff her feelings. "Not so modest, if you ask me, dearie."

Savannah clears her throat. "I'm willing to do this for free because I love my little church friend. Myrtle reminds me of my grandma; may she rest in peace."

Mrs. Forni directs her gaze at Myrtle. "What about your son Hank?"

She clutches the oversized purse on her lap. "What about him? He's got other things on his plate. He wants to stick me in a nursing home. I've lived in my home for sixty years now and plan to die there."

Mrs. Forni pauses. "May I suggest a convenience account, then?" She squirms ever so slightly in her chair. "It allows another person to write checks with your supervision, as you wish, but also provides … safeguards to your account. It protects your assets in the event of your death."

Alicia recalls the exasperation on Savannah's face when she returned from the bank with the old gal and Myrtle's new convenience account. Savannah now had access to her limited checking account but not the savings account. It meant their long game had to continue until Savannah could think of a way to gain access to the assets in Myrtle's savings account. The more time that passes in a long game, the easier it is for things to go wrong. It also meant that Alicia was dependent on her friend to share whatever small amounts of cash Savannah could siphon off over time.

It didn't sit well between the two thieves, and they began to quarrel.

Neither did Savannah not telling her the turtle was worth four million dollars until a month later. They spied on each other and took risks. Alicia pocketed the occasional piece of jewelry she hoped the turtle wouldn't miss, and Savannah helped herself to an antique set of silverware Myrtle hadn't used since she'd known her.

Greed and time took their toll. The pressure kept building.

For a week, they primed Myrtle to ask Mrs. Forni for a transfer of fifty thousand from savings to the new convenience account to pay for home renovations, but Myrtle blew the call; she just couldn't bring herself to ask for money. She didn't think she needed to spend that much money on the house. Mrs. Forni contacted Hank, who arrived at the house as Alicia's shift was ending, and Savannah pulled into the driveway right behind his Buick.

Seeing two strange cars and women in the drive, Hank ordered them to leave. Savannah protested, insisting she was Myrtle's caregiver from church, but when he dialed the police, Savannah jumped in her car and laid rubber leaving. Hearing the commotion from inside, Alicia considered Hank, a bulldog who'd arrived with fangs bared. She snatched up her belongings and sprinted to her SUV, which she found blocked by Hank's Buick. Panicked, she ran over Myrtle's rosebushes to reach the safety of the street while Hank ran after her. If the bulldog made her license plate, she was screwed.

Later that day, Hank drove Myrtle to the bank, where they learned that there was no person named 'Savannah Grimes'; the address, cell number, and all other information provided was phony. Hank chastised himself for missing the license plate when he filed the police report.

The convenience account was closed.

Hank's frustration at his mother's naivete was short-lived because Myrtle was inconsolable over the loss of her young caregivers and insisted they were good Christian girls. Hank estimated the two had made off with over six grand in cash and valuables, not counting the cash salaries Myrtle paid them over the months.

'Savannah' later told Alicia she learned from another church acquaintance that Hank stayed with his mother until he had to return to work. The private duty workers he hired didn't pan out, Myrtle's dementia worsened, and he placed her in a nursing home. During her first year there, she fell out of bed and broke a hip. A few months later, she died.

Almost home, Alicia shakes her head at the memory. She still blames Hank for Myrtle's death and the estrangement of her partner in crime.

Pulling into her gravel driveway, she pockets Barb's business card and decides to find out exactly what this peacock is willing to do to spread her wings and strut.

She fails to notice the nondescript Camry parked down the street with the same muscular and long-haired man behind the wheel. His fingers drum the steering wheel, exposing the jailhouse tattoos on his knuckles.

Sea Changes

"Young vampires are sexy—they live forever and remain
young and hot."

Barb

Today is Claire's thirty-fifth birthday, Barb's oldest child and only daughter, and the plan is for Claire to drive over for dinner after her work shift.

Barb cleans, shops, and cooks during the day. She bakes rosemary bread ahead of time and (at Claire's request) preps five ramekins of Crème Brule. She preps the boys' favorite appetizer, Clams Casino, so all that she must do is slide the Cherrystones under the broiler once the kids arrive. Then, she organizes a large charcuterie board bedecked with artisan cheeses, salamis, olives, veggies, crackers, and dipping sauces. The main entrée and side require negligible prep time.

The day begins well, the boys arrive first, and Barb is full of bubbly energy, eager to receive updates about their jobs and girlfriends.

Mathew, her older son, helps himself to a Diet Coke and a fistful of cashews before he plops down on the sofa and turns on a football game. "The I.T. job's okay. I should get a raise next month. My boss is kind of a dick, but hey, it's a paycheck. I don't wanna do this for the rest of my life. And I don't know about Marcy. I think she wants to get serious, but I'm not ready. Some weekends, I want to hang with my friends, play video games, and watch sports."

Barb shrugs at the disruption of the TV and uncorks a bottle of wine. "Marcy's a nice girl, but you're right. You shouldn't feel pressured to jump into a serious relationship at your age." She pauses to heave a dramatic sigh and the tone in her voice darkens. "About the job situation, my offer still stands. If you want to finish college, I'll pay for it, even though in the divorce settlement your father agreed to pay for your college. I held up my end of the agreement; I paid for your private high schools." She thinks this for the millionth time: the *best* he could do was two years of community college, the damn cheapskate.

The boys glance at each other and shift uncomfortably in their seats as if to say: *Here we go again.*

Gary takes a seat across from Barb with a barely audible groan and narrows his eyes at her. Her eyes narrow as she shoots him a quick look. She knows what he must be thinking—that every time she magnanimously offers to pay for something for *her* kids, the next day she asks him for money from his inheritance, even though they agreed his inheritance is set aside to supplement their retirement money, for they both are all too aware their adult children will not be there to help them in their old age.

She turns to her other son. "What about you, Mark?"

The younger son twists open a Bud and feeds Barb's terrier a slice of cheese from the table. "The company I work for won a painting contract with an apartment complex downtown. I was about to be laid off before that came through. Should be good for several more months of work."

Barb nods and drains her first glass of Zinfandel. "How is Denise?"

Translation: *how are you and Denise doing*? The boy's relationship histories with the fairer sex are, on the best of days, shaky.

Mathew grins and shoots Mark a knowing look, prodding him to spill the beans. "I didn't want to mention this because you'll overreact, but she had too much to drink after her shift ended the other night. We argued over her car keys, and when I took them, she hit me a couple of times. A cop cruising by saw the struggle and thought I was abusing her. He wanted to arrest me. She was belligerent. I swear to God, I never hit her; I blocked her blows and tried to pin her arms."

Barb leans forward in her chair. "That's awful! Goddamn cops. Did Denise tell the truth?"

"She didn't want to at first. She was in the driver's seat, and the cop could tell she was hammered. The engine was off, and the keys were in her hands—"

Mark seemed relieved when Barb's cell rang.

"Hi, hon. You almost here?" She rises and walks to the kitchen while Claire speaks to her on the other end.

Gary can tell from the slump of her shoulders and the hurt in her voice that Claire isn't coming and that Barb will wail and gnash her teeth over life's injustices the rest of the night.

From the other room, they hear, "But this was the time *you* said would work." Several curt *uh-huhs* follow until the call ends. The gas stove ignites with a whoosh, dishes clatter loudly, and Barb busies herself with the entrée and side dish.

Gary sees her reach for a Chardonnay refill as she calls out in a gruff voice, "Dinner will be ready in ten minutes." In a moment, the crying will begin soon if it hasn't already.

The boys shoot each other knowing glances and return their attention to the football game on TV.

Gary knows from experience a verbal response from him will only make things worse, but no response is just as bad, so he sits there in hellish limbo, waiting for the other shoe to drop.

Dinner is a tense, awkward affair, with seared sea scallops in garlic and white wine and white asparagus in Hollandaise sauce. Barb sits with rigid posture, her facial features stiff, and occasionally sighs and shoots off a few brief, barbed comments about Claire while the boys ignore her. Her sons read the mood around the table and, after dessert, speed away like bandits for the border.

Gary helps her transfer the leftover food and dirty plates from the dining room table to the island kitchen. He walks with his head down and waits for the inevitable implosion. Some days, it begins the moment the boys leave the house. The only certainty he knows is she will blow her stack over the latest perceived outrage at the hands of her daughter.

She refills her wine glass in the kitchen and places a hand on a hip. "You want to know why Claire didn't come?"

He dreads responding; he knows her answer will be a different variation on a recurring theme. Only the particulars change. It is exhausting, mind-numbing, and tedious. Every major holiday, birthday, and anniversary ends in drama. He doesn't remember a single happy get-together involving her kids since he's known her. It's like being strapped to a bomb. "Tell me."

"Her *daddy* (she says with the malice of a petulant teenager) hadn't seen her on her birthday, and she felt sorry for him since I have you, and he's all alone in his condo. Bullshit. She likes to twist the knife in me any chance she gets. That, and she wants to stay in his will."

Gary knows there is nothing he can say to console her, but if he says nothing, she will interpret it as not him caring, and then she'll redirect her anger toward him sooner rather than later. "Couldn't she have stopped here for dinner on the way to her father's?"

She takes a healthy pull from the wineglass, a brightly colored one with red glitter that spells out her name. She has four such wine glasses. "I suggested it, but her new boyfriend bought last-second tickets to a downtown show she wants to see." She heaves a heavy sigh. "Once again, no time for Mom. It's all about her, the bitch!"

He moves closer. "She shouldn't have gone back on her word after committing to the dinner." To mention Barb's kitchen work would only compound her pain.

She backs away from his offer of consolation, holding out a hand like a stop sign.

Then the tears flow, along with the mascara.

She drains her glass; her words to him begin to slur. "I didn't have to have her, you know. She was a mistake. I wasn't supposed to get pregnant so soon. I could have aborted her. I wanted to go to med school and become a doctor. *He* stayed in law school and started his legal career while I raised his three kids. I didn't start my RN program until the kids went to school because that's what *he* wanted. And the boys … they knew Claire had no intention to be here; I could read it in their faces. How quickly they left. They don't care about me, either; they blame me for the divorce."

Gary's heard the retaliatory angry abortion story countless times and knows from past episodes this wallowing will last for days, and she will be inconsolable. He shuts his eyes and does the math again—her divorce was eighteen years ago.

On other major holidays and birthdays, her boys take turns being the heavy. If not, it's her boss, a co-worker, her elderly mother, or one of her emotionally damaged siblings.

Later tonight, her anger over Claire's perceived selfishness and insensitivity finally shifts fully to her ex-husband/lawyer for poisoning her children against her, and finally, the anger lands on Gary for not being supportive enough. She will call him horrible names and then want him to cuddle with her all night. This is a fact, not a possibility.

She fishes out prescription bottles from her purse and dry swallows some pills. Likely lithium and her anti-anxiety medication.

Persistent Gary wants, somehow, to help. "Leave the dishes; I'll clean the kitchen. Dinner was great. You want to soak in the tub or lay down?"

Her nose runs, and her cheeks are red. "I was a good Mom! I was a good Mom!" Her speech slurs more as she endlessly repeats one of her favorite mantras. She's beside herself, a modern-day martyr.

She throws the colander into the sink with such force it bounces and rattles with a metallic clang that startles Gary. It breaks a plate in the sink, and when Barb leaves the kitchen, she yanks the chain that hangs from the light fixture above the island with such force it breaks the three-way switch. During past fits, she's thrown glasses to the floor, removed family pictures from their frames, and cut off the offending child's face. She once screamed at him for having the audacity of keeping the occasional photo of women he used to date years ago, harping on it so incessantly that he eventually threw out all the pictures, which he now regrets.

"Dammit, Barb! I know you're upset, but destroying shit does no good. I'm tired of fixing all the things you break."

She retraces her steps and wheels on him, her jaw set. "Fuck you! You don't care about me. Go to hell!"

"I can't talk with you when you get in these moods. Go upstairs and sleep it off."

"Forget the dishes. Come to bed with me. I need you to hold me."

Experience tells him all this accomplishes is her retelling the sad, sordid story of her first marriage over and over in a whiny, drunken loop. He shakes his head. "I will clean the kitchen. I swear to God, this happens every damn holiday or birthday."

"Fine. I hate you, you bastard."

"Sleep … it … off."

"FUCK YOU!"

"You promised when we married, you'd no longer obsess about your first marriage and not get so worked up over stuff that happened twenty years ago. I know kids complicate divorce, but they're adults now. Every Christmas, every birthday, you try to buy their love with thousands of dollars in gifts. It doesn't work. You bend over backward for them, and do they care? No. You asked me to cut a check to Claire from my parents' estate for thirty thousand dollars. Why? For one of the worst possible reasons a parent (or step-parent) wants to hear is that a thirty-five-year-old woman has *no clue* how her credit card debt got that high. She makes more money than you do, and she's single! That came two days after I buried my mother, but I wrote the check. In return, Claire couldn't even spend a few hours here. They're playing you. I will not keep doing this."

"I hate you so much. You want a divorce? Fine. You file."

Another of her favorite mantras. He bends to retrieve a clean washrag and sighs. "You're drunk. Go to bed."

She flips him the finger as she stomps up the stairs, which creaks under her weight.

While he picks shards of broken plates from the garbage disposal, stores the leftovers, and washes dishes, he looks back on the last few years. They met at the hospital; she was a high-energy nurse new on the rehab floor, and he was a pharmacy supervisor. The attraction was mutual—they dated six months before eloping, mostly because it was a second marriage for both, and neither could tolerate the other's family. She was fun in the beginning, the sex was hot, and they worked to cultivate mutual interests. He'd witnessed mild tension with her kids before they married, but nothing that approached the current level of melodrama. He attributed it to her worsening bipolar depression, and the more she drank, the more unstable she became. Something more sinister seems to be brewing in her; he can't put his finger on it. She refuses to see the therapist her shrink recommended. She claims she knows more than any therapist and they don't help.

He pulls a clean bed sheet from the dryer and readies the couch in front of the television.

Hours later, he wakes when Barb curls up next to him, whispers a half-assed apology in his ear, and wants to have sex.

He removes her hand from his penis and props himself on an elbow. "No. You can't simply say you're sorry after you say all this hateful shit and expect me to forget about it. How many times have I left work early due to your emotional crises? Because one of your kids or your brother either said something stupid to you on the phone, or you think your boss is an idiot or doesn't respect you enough, or some cruel thing your mother said. If I leave work early again, my boss will write me a final warning. You need to regain control of your emotions."

She stares into his blue eyes. "So, what if you lose your job? I'd choose you over my job every time if you were having problems. Because *I* care about you."

"Did you hear what you just said? That's sick."

"No, it isn't. It's true."

"You switch jobs every other year or so, either because you can't stand your boss or you think you know more than the doctors, or you refuse to work with another line nurse, or you job hop to collect the 5K bonus because of the nursing shortage. I'm surprised you haven't switched jobs since we married. You're burning bridges with every hospital system in town."

"I need you to hold me."

The wall clock reads four a.m. "You're off today. I must get up in two hours for work. I'm going upstairs. To *sleep*. Stay here."

An eye roll, and then the television winks on. As he closes the bedroom door behind him, he hears familiar dialogue from a *True Blood* rerun, her favorite show.

She lays down on the sofa and masturbates to a sex scene between Sookie and Bill, anticipating when Eric will make his appearance on screen. Her troubles are forgotten for now by a vicarious desire to live forever, and most importantly, to always remain young and beautiful. She climaxes when Eric appears on the screen.

Improper Dinner Talk at Christmas

"Most people turn a blind eye to the sick truth about bears
and chimpanzees."

Alicia

She trudges up five flights of stairs in the poorly lit
Terrace Arms housing project and intentionally arrives thirty
minutes late after the meal begins. Her younger step-brother
Tyler and step-sister Missy sit stiffly around the table and,
as expected, give no acknowledgment of her arrival. She
places a brown paper bag that contains a bottle of
Peppermint Schnapps and a carton of Kools next to her
mother's full plate.

She catches her breath for a moment while she weighs
her words. "Merry Christmas, Jean. I didn't wrap these
because last year you bitched about me wasting paper."

Jean makes a dismissive motion with her hand and rises
to find an extra plate and silverware, telling the others to
make room around the small oak kitchen table. A plume of
cigarette smoke trails in her wake.

Alicia turns on the ceiling fan while Jean has her back
turned. "Two dudes, one black and one white, tried to accost
me at the third-floor landing on my way up. On your floor, a
Mexican wanted to sell me drugs. When are you gonna find
a better place to live, Jean? That damn elevator hasn't
worked for years now, and you, with your bad leg and all."

Jean busies herself with making a plate of spaghetti and
meatballs, topping the jiggly red mess off with two cold
slices of garlic bread before she sets it in front of the empty
spot at the table.

Alicia pulls over the fourth chair while she observes the physical changes since the last visit: the weight gain, the bags under the eyes, and the gray hair. "I see you stopped coloring your hair and resumed smoking."

Jean lights another cigarette and glares at her oldest. "I'm too old to play the game. No one's going to jump me or offer to sell drugs to an old broad like me."

"When will the absentee slumlord fix the elevator, Jean?"

She gets the same dismissive hand wave in return that she remembers from when she was a little girl. As if to say: *don't bother me, I got my own problems.*

They eat in silence. The step-kids go back for seconds. Alicia picks at the cold food and finishes her first beer before her mother speaks again.

"I say I'll find a better place when my oldest starts helping her mother financially every month."

Ty and Missy whisper and smile at each other. They've heard or suspected something is up, the little shits.

"I'm on Medicaid disability, Jean. Remember? The state barely gives me a pot to piss in."

Jean puts down her fork. "Same as me. I got no pension, and the worthless daddy of those two," she said, pointing across the table, "left me nothing but bills to pay before he ran off with some cheap whore. Served him right to get the cancer and die."

Ty breaks wind in response and offers an insincere apology. Missy giggles and stares at Jean, defiant.

Alicia wheels on them. "Ty and Missy, how old are you assholes now? Twenty-two, twenty-three? Start acting like it."

They avert their eyes and withdraw inward. Alicia is the Alpha female between the three, and they know it. The wail of a siren on the street below is all the excuse Ty needs to rush to the window and watch for the destination of the ambulance. This time it speeds past the high-rise.

The silence resumes, and Alicia polishes off her second and third beers before dessert. When everyone finishes their slice of a previously frozen Mrs. Smith's apple pie with fake whipped cream, Jean orders the step-kids to clear the table and watch television.

She lights a cigarette and turns to Alicia. "I meant what I said. I think $500 a month is a fair place to start. For now."

Alicia doesn't bother to hide her shock or anger. She pulls Jean's ashtray closer, lights her own cigarette, and waits until she can speak in a calm voice. "First off, I don't have that kind of money, and even if I did, what makes you think I'd give it to you?"

Jean laughs, and flicks ash into the tray. "It's a small town. I hear things. I have friends who look out for me; they tell me things about you ..."

"You heard wrong. What little money I have after food and bills goes into rehabbing—"

She leans forward to stare into Alicia's eyes. "Stop. No more song and dance about the house. Don't bullshit a bullshitter. We're cut from the same dirty cloth."

"I don't know what you're talking a—"

"A friend ran into your old prison buddy, the one with all the aliases, at a bar. You never told me you two had such a falling out; as I recall, you were thick as thieves, and my friend got an earful of the whole story. *Samantha* or *Savannah* or whatever she calls herself today must be one of those unfortunate souls who can't handle her liquor." Jean smiles that lazy, knowing smile of hers through the smoke around the table. "There's more. The other day, a friend of mine called. Billie Lee works at the concierge desk at a casino halfway across the state. Says I need to listen close. Tells me a fascinating story about a robbery in their hotel, and the suspect is female. The hotel manager shows every concierge worker the security footage and asks if anyone remembers checking in the woman on camera into the hotel or seeing her. The robber reportedly told the mark that she was a stewardess sharing a room with other stews. Lo and behold, the woman in the picture is you under a big floppy hat! At least you tried to avoid the cameras. My friend called me so I could warn you.

"Consider yourself warned. Feel free to use me as an alibi. That'll be five hundred bucks, please."

Alicia freezes for a moment, unsure of how to respond. She curses to herself how damn small the world can be, even when she hunts far from home.

The knowing smile returns. She taps ash into the tray. "My casino friend's a good egg. Don't worry; she's keeping her pie hole shut at work. Just so you know, she said your John or mark or whatever you call them decided not to go to the cops. That alone is worth the first $500. Be a damn shame if my friend's conscience gets the better of her one day. I think the number is a fair price … so you can stay in your little home, *rehabbing* …" She rolls her eyes when she says the word. "Rather than go back to jail." She folds her arms. "How much did you scam from him?"

From the living room, Ty and Missy argue over the remote. There's a brief tussle, someone gets hit, and Missy whimpers. Jean smirks.

Alicia rises and pokes her head into the living room. The fight is over, and order is restored on the couch. Alicia stands behind Jean's chair and lowers her face close to her ear before she speaks. "After what that bastard did, you'd rat me out?"

Jean swivels in the chair to face her. "Hey, we do what we gotta do. I'm not young like you. I can't hook a man to pay the bills and I sure as hell don't want to work. Look at this as a win-win situation. I teach you some tricks you don't know, and in return, you help me leave this rat-infested hole."

The thought of choking Jean flashes through her mind, but she picks up the bottle of Schnapps and lets it fall from her hand. It explodes on the kitchen vinyl. Ty and Missy rush in and watch the sweet, syrupy mess spread toward the slippers on Jean's feet. The smell of peppermint overpowers the stale smell of the kitchen.

"I'm glad you two are back. Sit down."

Ty and Missy look to their mom for guidance, and when no direction comes, they retake their seats, surprised to see Jean is now being the Alpha female of the entire family.

Alicia slowly walks around the circular table. "I'm gonna tell you a story."

Jean stares hard at her. "Don't you dare!"

She kicks shards of glass away as she takes her seat and stares at Jean. "Ty, Missy, you like polar bears? They're cute, right?"

Not knowing what else to do, they shrug.

"Did you know that polar bears, both mothers and fathers, sometimes eat their babies?"

They make confused, disgusted faces.

"When there's no other food available, or if they sense the babies are born deformed or sickly, they eat their young."

They don't know what to say. Jean sits frozen, listening intently.

Alicia turns to Ty and Missy. "You like monkeys and chimps? They eat their young, too. When male monkeys take over a territory, they eat any babies in the new pride so they can reproduce with the females. If an alpha monkey suspects he isn't the father of a baby, he often eats it. He does this by sucking the brains from the baby—"

Jean's hand strikes the table with a bang. "This is not proper dinner talk."

Alicia's eyes remain on her step-siblings. "There ain't a lot of difference between these mammals and humans. Brain stems, warm-blooded, central nervous systems. Dinner's over, Jean. This is the educational part of our Christmas celebration this year. The real circle of life, if you will."

Ty leans forward in his seat. "What about mother monkeys?"

"Glad you asked. I was getting to that. Infanticide by cannibalism is a more common practice in the primate world than people think. Some species of mother monkeys are more dependent on the pride to help raise their babies. Some give birth to multiple babies that grow too large for the mother to carry around. If they don't receive enough help from the pride, some mothers eat their young."

Jean's face is a perplexed frown. "Are you done? Are you happy now?"

"Almost. Ty, Missy, did either of you feel like one of those baby bears or monkeys when you were young in the old house?"

They glance at Jean for help, which never comes before Ty shakes his head uncertainly while a tear falls to Missy's cheek.

Alicia rises from the chair and grabs her purse. "Well, I did." To Jean: "You'll have my decision by the weekend." Then to all: Merry Fucking Christmas and to all, a goodnight!"

As she closes the front door and prepares to run the gauntlet of dealers and creeps who lean against the darkened stairwells, Jean orders Missy to fetch the mop and clean the mess on the kitchen floor. Missy's cries escalate to sobs. They echo in Alicia's ears all the way to her SUV.

Look Who's Coming for More Than Dinner?

"After all I sacrificed for her, Claire can be replaced."

Barb

The day after Christmas, Barb broached the subject with Gary of Alicia spending time in their home between now and New Year's. "I feel bad for her. She's got an illness that could kill her at any time, and her family is a bloody trainwreck. She has no one else. This would mean a lot to me and to her. Just until we go back to work after the New Year."

Gary's gut response is he hates the idea and prepares for a battle. "You don't know this woman. What is this health issue that she has? What if something happens while she's here and what's your boss and the hospital going to say if something happens to a patient in our home?"

She makes a face and huffs. "She has a brain aneurysm we're monitoring. 2.6 right now. Not close to requiring surgery. She also has a rare blood disorder. Work doesn't need to know, and if for some reason they find out or something happens, I will get another job. It isn't hurting anyone."

"It isn't? Does that mean you already invited her?"

Her hands go to her hips. "I did. She'll be here for dinner tonight. You said you've got plans with your friends this week, and after the Christmas debacle with my kids, this is exactly the pick-me-up I need. You don't have to entertain her or change your plans. It also means you'll eat great meals when she's here."

Typical, he tells himself. *She's scouting for a project, someone else to love her, since her daughter Claire isn't showing her the amount of love she expects.*

"What's her name, and how old is she?"

"Alicia. She's 32."

A few years younger than Claire. A 'replacement' daughter. "Anything else I should know about her?"

"She's gorgeous. I think she and Mark could be a good match. He always falls for good-looking, empty-headed bartenders with drinking problems. Alicia has her own home and is rehabbing it herself. She's self-reliant."

At least the part about Mark's girlfriends is true. "Does Alicia know this?"

She shakes her head. "We're having shrimp scampi, artichoke salad, and molten lava cakes tonight, around six." Then she walks to the kitchen.

Gary sits reading in their study when a white SUV rattles to a stop in front of their home. Several inches of snow have fallen this afternoon, and more is expected. He waits until the noise dies down before walking downstairs.

To his surprise, a pit bull chases their two terriers around the living room while Barb and Alicia are in the kitchen. Alicia is nearly six feet tall, has long, straight strawberry blond hair well past her ass, but likely weighs close to 200 pounds, and her face is rather plain. The pit bull sees Gary enter the room and interrupts the chase to bark at him.

He stares at his wife. *Great. Barb didn't mention anything about a monster dog,* he says to himself. Barb drinks wine and Alicia twists open a diet soda during the pandemonium.

After the introductions, Barb says, "I told Alicia she could bring Jack rather than leave him alone in her home for days. We have a fenced yard, after all."

"But one with a short fence that's perfect to keep our smaller dogs in, but not a tall one like Jack," Gary says.

"Well, then get that stake from the garage and screw it into the ground. We can put Jack on the leash when he needs to pee."

"It's been in the twenties. The ground is frozen."

Barb shoots him a look. "Get the dog set up, then we can eat."

Gary finally manages to screw the stake into the ground, and once on the leash, Jack pisses on his BBQ grill cover like there's no tomorrow. Gary looks on as the dog yanks the corkscrew stake from the ground and easily jumps the fence. The only thing that saves Gary is the trailing rope eventually gets wrapped around a neighbor's tree two blocks away. He walks Jack back home, and the dog growls at him the entire way.

Barb and Alicia are oblivious to the goings on outside, and when Gary returns, the food is on the table. Barb glares at him and says Grace (she only does this when they have company), and they dig in.

Alicia turns to him. "You have a beautiful home. Thank you both for inviting me."

"You're welcome," Gary says. "Barb tells me you have a home and are rehabbing it yourself."

She actually pays others to do the work, but Barb doesn't need to know the truth. "It's been a long, slow process, especially with my health and scarcity of money, but it is fun. I'm currently putting down a wooden, tongue-and-groove floor in the living room. The house is over a hundred years old. It's what I like to do. I will continue to be an independent, self-sufficient woman as long as my health allows. Some days, I move a little slower and must stop to take care of myself.

"This dinner is fabulous. The shrimp is perfect. Barb, you are a great cook!"

Barb can't hide the blush that spreads across her face even though she knows she's a great cook. She happily accepts the compliment.

After dinner, Gary offers to do the dishes while the women sit in the family room and gossip about the hospital. Barb asks how the visit with her mother went. Alicia shakes her head and feigns tears. "She wants financial help from me to move into a better apartment, but she knows I don't have that kind of extra money. She just doesn't understand. She can be so mean." She turns to Barb. "Mothers and daughters—a never-ending war, it seems."

That sets off Barb in dissing Claire. Right on cue, from Alicia's perspective, given past remarks she'd heard from Barb at the hospital.

Gary's eyes narrow and focus on Barb. He misses Alicia's subtle grin.

The women turn on a popular TV show about celebrity dancing, and Barb asks Gary to walk Jack and let their dogs out. It beats watching a dance show. Jack urinates another river-like stream on his BBQ cover. When he returns, he tells Alicia that her SUV needs to be moved as their side has no parking and the street is a snow route. Barb suggests Gary move the vehicle and Alicia tosses the keys at him without a thank you.

Gary puts his coat back on and trudges out in the falling snow. The SUV won't start, and he returns with this info.

"It probably needs a jump because of the weather," Alicia says, without taking her eyes off the screen.

Gary doesn't bother to ask whether she has cables. He enters the garage, pulls his car out, starts the SUV with his own set of cables, parks it across from their house on the correct side, and then returns his car to the garage. "Guess she didn't see the NO PARKING sign on our side of the street," he mumbles to himself. Cold, he enters the kitchen to make himself an Irish hot chocolate and finds the women making a batch of brownies.

Alicia hands him one on a paper plate and gives him a wink. "It's a special recipe."

The women find a chick flick to watch, and Gary retreats to the study to drink scotch and read. Sometime later, the words on the page he's reading begin to float off into space, and he feels tense and paranoid. A tightness fills his chest, and he has a headache. He walks to the living room and asks what is in the brownie, even though he knows.

Alicia looks at Barb and says, "You said you told him."

Barb giggles and spills red wine on the rug. "I forgot!" The giggles are replaced by raucous laughter. Her eyes grow wide as saucers. "Pot! The other day you and I talked about trying it again when we retire because we hadn't had any since college. Alicia brought some over. Wasn't that nice?"

"Last time I checked, we're not retired, and you know THC stays in the body a long time. The hospital does occasional drug tests, Barb."

She repeats his last sentence in a mocking tone, which sparks more laughter from the women on the couch.

He returns to the study with a glass of water and two aspirin but can no longer focus on reading. Marijuana must be a lot stronger now than when I was in college; he says to himself as he lies down on a sofa. The paranoia lasts all night and into the morning. *If this woman is so sick, what is she doing ingesting marijuana?*

Meanwhile, the wine/pot party continues full-time in the living room. Alicia moves next to her on the sofa while Barb plans tomorrow. "We're going to get mani-pedis and lunch at my favorite place before we hit the grocery store. I'm thinking of a rack of lamb with Brussels sprouts for dinner. Gary loves lamb."

Alicia has formed tentative opinions on their relationship and wants to test them out to find vulnerabilities. "He seems a little uptight, even after the brownie."

"He's a bit old before his time, I admit, but he has his uses."

An odd choice of words, Alicia thinks and smiles when she asks, "And what are they?"

"He makes good money, he's got a large inheritance, and he's a saver while I'm a spender."

"So, he's got money. How is he in the sack?"

"That's rather personal."

She massages Barb's shoulder. "Sorry. I thought we were being upfront here."

"He may have lost some interest in the bedroom. He's had some health issues that compromise his ability sometimes."

The massage intensifies. "Want another brownie?"

Barb shakes her head. "I'm feeling a bit jumpy. It doesn't make me feel as good as I remember. I need some water." She walks to the kitchen and fetches a bottle. "Do you use pot regularly? It's not good for your condition."

Alicia pretends to be absorbed by the TV show before she uses the bathroom.

During the next two days, Barb and Alicia get their nails done and a deep tissue massage at Barb's expense. One night, Gary plays poker at a friend's house, and the second day, he goes bird hunting. He returns from a farmer's property in Illinois with a pheasant and four quail, then locks his shotgun with his other weapons in a basement safe. Barb refuses to dress anything he shoots, but she does a good job cooking the birds.

Alicia refuses to try the game after Barb finds a piece of buckshot in her pheasant. Barb gives her leftovers from the racks of lamb.

Alicia shakes her head and turns to Gary. "I don't know how you can shoot those poor little birds. It would make me so sad."

Barb gives him a subtle shake of her head.

"It's a skill not everyone can do or has the stomach for. They taste great, but to each his own," Gary says and smiles to himself when he wonders whether their guest has the faintest clue how the poor lamb was slaughtered.

Barb passes her the mashed potatoes. "Gary used to hunt and fish with his father when he was a teenager. He retreats frequently to the basement to make his own bullets and flies for his fishing rods."

She makes a mental note to check their basement. A look of distaste remains on Alicia's face. "Do you hunt and fish with him?"

"Hell, no."

"Guns make me nervous. Never held or fired one," Alicia says, lying through her teeth. "They're used too often to kill innocent people."

Gary finishes his plate, thanks Barb for cooking the game just right, and heads for the door to take out Jack and their dogs. He will have the cobbler and ice cream later by himself in the study.

As before, Jack pisses for what seems like minutes on his BBQ grill cover while their dogs roam free in the fenced backyard. "You know you can pee on the backyard grass rather than my grill," he tells the guest dog. Jack has been friendly enough with their dogs, playing and chasing them on and off the living room sectionals, but he at times snaps at Gary's hand, especially when given a treat. The dog has heterochromic eyes, weighs eighty pounds, and pulls like an Iditarod sled dog on his leash.

Before bed that night, Gary sits while Jack chases their dogs over the sofa grouping. Jack lands hard on his inner thigh before he pushes off to resume the chase. Gary's leg hurts, and when he inspects it in the bathroom, the skin is broken through his jeans, and a large, hardened mass has already formed. Barb looks at it and suggests he get a carotid Doppler tomorrow to check for a DVT since he's had many surface ones after a heavy section of fence landed on his leg and ankle years ago.

While Gary does this the next day, Barb takes Alicia to lunch and then to the grocery store.

A DVT is found that has moved to his left groin. He's told that it could move from there to his heart or brain and potentially be fatal. His doctor places him on Warfarin. He will need to take it for 6-8 months to help break up the clot. When he tells the women this, Barb says, "See, I thought so!" while Alicia says nothing.

Gary steams over what he perceives is Alicia's unconcerned attitude about what happened to him. Though he knows it was an accident, he feels he deserves an apology or at least some recognition from Alicia. What he gets is Jack's leash handed to him by Barb so he can walk her dog after dinner.

Gary goes to bed early while Barb entertains her guest in the living room. While he walks the stairs to the second floor, he overhears Alicia saying to Barb, "Is he mad at me? I don't think he likes me."

He hears a portion of his wife's response. "…he turns into a baby when he gets sick."

He's ready for the week to end, eager to return to work and be rid of this unwanted house guest of Barb's in two more days.

❁   ❁   ❁

Alicia has been watching and formulating opinions about Barb and her marital relationship since she's been in their home. A peacock appears to be the right animal to describe her hostess. One that is at home is aggressive but also does not have good self-esteem. One who easily gets her feathers ruffled and one who is used to getting her way. She imagines this peacock has a hole inside her that she's trying to fill with love and recognition and, perhaps, something else. It's a matter of how far Alicia's willing to go to find out what she really wants in life.

Barb opens another wine bottle, and Alicia cracks open another soda while they watch the latest popular chick series on television. Barb begins to slur her words after downing half the bottle while she again recaps her frustration with her grown children.

"Gary recently inherited a sizable amount of money after his parents died, and he plans to retire soon."

"That's lucky for him."

"Yeah. Lucky for him," Barb says sardonically.

Alicia keeps her eyes on the screen. "Trouble in paradise?"

Barb refills her glass and hiccups. "He won't give my boys a penny to help with their business or college."

"I thought you said he paid off your daughter's credit card debts, like twenty-five grand?"

She nods. "She paid him back about a third of it until he made me angry one day, and I told her the debt was forgiven. Even *that* earned me zero brownie points with Claire, the cold bitch. My kids hate me."

Alicia turns to face her inebriated hostess, thinking now is the time. "So, what do you want in life?"

"I want to retire and live off his inheritance until we're old enough for Medicare. I don't want to work anymore. I worked my entire adult life helping people. I want us to travel and spend money on the kids rather than squirrel it away for some rainy day that may never come. I keep telling Gary he can't take it with him when he dies, but he counters with the fact that none of the kids will help us in our old age, which is true."

Alicia moves closer to Barb on the sofa, so close their knees and shoulders touch.

When a sex scene comes on the screen that involves two women, Alicia asks, "Have you ever been with a woman?"

"A drunken kegger in college once. Why?"

"I think women know how to make love far better than most men."

Barb places her glass on the table. "That's probably true. Does that mean you're lesbian?"

Alicia rubs her hand through Barb's short pixie cut with blonde highlights. "I've found experience and enthusiasm are more important than merely having a penis or male handsomeness or feminine beauty."

Barb remembers her plan to set up Alicia with her younger son. "You still haven't answered my question."

"I'm bi-sexual." Alicia kisses her on the mouth. The kiss deepens, their arms explore one another, and when Alicia starts to remove her hostess's sweater, Barb pulls away and rises.

"Gary's upstairs." Barb clears her throat. "It's getting late. I'm drunk and need to go to bed. You know where the guest bedroom is. There are fresh towels and a robe for you in the bedroom."

Barb hurries for the steps and calls goodnight over her shoulder.

The Man at the Top of the Stairs

"Monsters can be anybody and everywhere."

Alicia

Barb and Gary's guest room is twice the size of her bedroom at home. She brushes her teeth and throws the tacky decorative pillows to the floor before she climbs under the comforter and sheet. She stares at the large ocean print on the opposite wall while she weighs out how to play this and for how much. A short-term score of guns, jewelry, and cash, or could she pull off a long game for an even greater reward? Both will likely be tricky and, given the suspicious husband, filled with confrontation and emotion, unless a weakness of his can be put into play. Seduction? Anger? Jealousy?

While she considers options and their associated risks and rewards, she gradually drifts to sleep.

In a dream she's transported to another house, far smaller and much less fancy. She's eleven years old. The first thing she sees is the Kit-Kat clock on the wall, the smiling black cat with a wagging tail and eyes that move left to right. Nowadays, you can find them mostly in antique or junk stores. It's a rare happy remembrance from childhood. It's on a cracked wall in the tiny bedroom downstairs where she liked to sleep in the summer because it was cooler.

In those distant days, Jean was less jaded and worked two jobs, one as a waitress and one as a dry cleaner's assistant. She was tall and thin back then and carried herself in a graceful manner. She thought her mother was beautiful but that she always seemed in search of something outside herself, or another person, to give her life meaning. She came home from work tired but managed to cook hamburger helper or sloppy joes for them, and they occasionally went to church on Sundays until that day when she was eleven.

Her father, Roscoe, a stocky Italian, was a veteran who worked sporadically after his tour. He was a smooth talker with big dreams of starting his own security company. She heard their neighbors sometimes refer to him as *the sponge* because Jean was the family breadwinner. Her mother told her he has PTSD from the army, and that is why he struggles to find and keep a job. He would share his dreams and plans for the family with Alicia when he was feeling upbeat or when he drank, usually when Jean was at work.

Since she was eight years old, she'd heard her parents argue more at night. Mom and Dad both seemed to withdraw from her and stay away from home more. Her older brother Ray was always out raising hell in the neighborhood with his friends. Alicia felt so alone at times she felt like an abandoned child, so she became an A student, played sports, and hung out at her friends' homes.

One summer night, when she was eleven, and Jean was at work, the other side of her bed creaked, and the mattress sank. Her father was in her bed, and on her nightstand was a sandwich and a glass of milk. Earlier that day, she had argued with her parents to buy her a cell phone because all her friends had phones, but they refused, and the words grew heated. She ran down to her room and stayed there, missing dinner.

"I brought you dinner," he said.

She wanted to ask why he was in her bed, but the smell of alcohol on his breath stopped her. She associated the smell with him becoming angry, which often resulted in her Mom being hit.

In a shaky voice, she said, "Are you going to hit me?"

He smiled at her, his eyes a bit glassy-eyed. "No, I'd never do that. You still want the cell phone?"

Her voice catches in her throat, but she manages an "Mm-hmm."

"I tell you what, you do something for me this week, and I will buy the phone for you. If you don't tell your mom about this, then I will give you the phone. Make sure you hide it from her. She finds it, and that's the end of it. She can never know about our deal, okay?"

She remembers wanting the phone more than anything so far in her life.

She mumbles a hesitant, "Okay."

The covers go over their heads, and he grabs her right hand and guides it over his body (which she finds is naked!) until he settles it on his penis. He instructs her what to do with her hand. He starts to moan and moves closer to her before he pushes her head into his lap. The covers make seeing difficult, and it's harder for her to breathe. The air is hot and stifling. More instructions about how to use her mouth follow. There's more urgency to his movements and he starts to groan. He pushes her head down onto him so hard she gags until he apologizes and releases his pressure. His legs thrust and twitch, and he moans for her to keep sucking. His body spasms, and he says, "Yes, yes! Now swallow what's in your mouth."

She does as she's told. He's her Dad, after all.

"Lick the water off and swallow again." More shuddering from him.

She remembers the bitter taste isn't like water. He places her hand again on his now soft penis and tells her to stroke it.

She does.

"Very good. We do this every night this week and on Monday I will buy your phone. Think of a hiding place for it, and above all, do not mention any of this to your mom. She won't understand. Are we absolutely clear about this? If she finds out, you'll be in big trouble, and you will never get a phone."

Alicia was scared and excited, and ashamed because it felt wrong, dirty. "I understand. Mom cannot know about this. If she does, I lose my phone."

"Very good. I know we're both sweaty right now, but keep the covers over your head until I go back upstairs. If you want dessert after dinner, there's leftover chocolate cake on the kitchen table."

He was true to his word. The man at the top of the stairs came to her room each night and on Monday gave her a shiny new black phone.

"Take good care of it. It wasn't cheap. You lose it, and that's all she wrote."

She nods.

The first week, she asked him for a phone case that she saw and wanted on-line. After another nighttime visit from Dad, she received the money to buy it.

Over the next year, when she wanted something that she suspected her mom would not approve of, the money was in her hands the next morning after a visit from Dad the night before.

It all ended the night mom found the stash when she cleaned the basement. Hidden in a metal strongbox under an old blanket by the furnace, she found the phone, over a hundred dollars, birth control pills, and a box of condoms. The phone had a code lock, but given the boy band case cover, she knew it must be Alicia's.

She told Roscoe about what she'd found. He acted shocked but didn't say much other than they should wait until tomorrow to confront her, given the late hour. Jean insisted they wake her now.

Jean didn't mention the box at first. Last year, Alicia had gradually cut back her participation in sports and spending time with her friends to almost nothing now. Her grades gradually dropped from A's to mostly C's. Jean thought she'd finally get some answers about Alicia's steady decline. She asked if there was anything wrong at school.

"I keep telling you there's nothing different at middle school other than I've lost interest in some of the classes."

"What about after school? Issues with friends? A boyfriend?"

She looks at the floor. "No one's bullying me. I don't like sports as much as I used to, and I do not have a boyfriend."

Jean pulls the phone, condoms, and pills from her pocket and places them on the table. "I found these in the basement. Explain."

She stirs in her chair, uneasy. She nods, still looking at the floor. Part of her wants to leave the family and run away, and part of her wants all this out in the open, even though it can never be undone. Alicia sneaks subtle looks at her dad that she hopes mom cannot see.

Of course, Jean sees.

"What do you know about this?" She asks her husband.

When he doesn't answer, she turns back to her daughter. "You better not lie to me, or I swear to God, I will beat you bloody for the first time!"

Alicia realizes she should have told them she found the phone on the street a few days ago, but that ship has sailed. "Me and my friends use the condoms to make water balloons."

Jean looks as if she's about to lose her mind. She reminds herself she should have had the sex talk with her before now, but it's back to the crisis at hand. "You're a damn liar. Kids use cheap balloons for water bombs. What about the birth control pills? Who are you having sex with? Is it that boy in your class that you like, Johnny Pritchard?"

Alicia has reached another crossroads in her young life. While Roscoe surreptitiously nods his head for her to agree with her mom, she glances at her dad while a scowl forms on her brow. "It isn't Johnny or any boy from school." She turns and glares at her dad while silent tears run down her cheeks.

She looks between the two of them and says, "I need to hear you say it."

She points at her dad when the tears roll down. "It's Roscoe." She gulps hard. "He made me do this in exchange for the cell phone last year. Then he forced me to have sex with him when you weren't here or in the mood. The birth control and condoms were my idea, paid for with *my* money." She feels ready to faint from the release of pent-up emotion, but then a wave of relief washes over her, thinking this nightmare will finally end.

Without a word, Jean picks up the metal box from the table, swings it in a fast motion, and bashes Roscoe's head with it. Jean follows with a flurry of epithets and her parents fall off their chairs onto the floor, physically fighting. Jean is more than holding her own, thanks to adrenaline.

Alicia doesn't say a word but unlocks her phone to dial 911. She tells the dispatcher their address and, eight minutes later, opens the front door. Jean's blouse is ripped open, and she has a cut near her scalp that bleeds onto her face. Roscoe's face has multiple fingernail scratches, his mouth and nose are bleeding, and there's a dinner knife stuck in his back. The cops take their statements and escort Roscoe into the back of the cruiser because Jean wants to press charges. She tells the officers she doesn't want him back in their house and that if he ever returns, she will kill him.

During this, Alicia has been straightening the mess in the basement. When the cops leave at 3 am, Jean talks with Alicia in her parents' bed and tries to reassure her that she can come to her for help with any problem. Before sleep overcomes them, Jean strokes her hair and asks, "Why was one of the kitchen knives downstairs?"

"I was going to kill him the next time he came for me from the top of the stairs." She steels herself and asks, "Where's the money that I earned?"

Jean looks stunned. "You're kidding, right? That you *earned* from being a whore? From not telling me what you were doing in my own home? It's part of the household money now. Kiss it goodbye, little girl."

Jean divorced Roscoe a few months later. When older brother Ray finally learned what happened, he threatened to kill his dad if he ever set foot in the house again. Jean and Alicia grew closer the next year until Jean started feeling lonely and stayed away from home to look for another husband. Her drinking increased, as did her time away from

Alicia. By this time, Ray had moved into a tiny apartment with his then-girlfriend.

The next year, Jean married Stan, a childless Catholic widower whose first wife couldn't get pregnant. He convinced Jean to have a child with him, but as fate would have it, she became pregnant two years in a row, and Tyler and Missy joined the family. Stan's saving grace was he held a steady job as a mailman. He was tall and thin, with a pencil-thin mustache. He seemed to accept Alicia, and she liked the fact that Stan held a steady job for the US mail, which lessened the financial responsibility on Jean, but over time she began to think of her new step-father as a player. She noticed how he looked and smiled at neighborhood women and casually flirted and followed them as they walked down the street.

Alicia moved out after high school and found a one-bedroom apartment she paid for at first by dealing drugs. When that proved too dangerous, she returned to sleeping with men for money. After several beatings, a friend introduced her to the confidence game.

She told herself: there will never be another man at the top of the stairs looking down at me.

A Malingerer and a Patient

"Nobody knows how I feel but me. I'm not crazy."

Alicia

Gary returns home late the next afternoon with Warfarin, which he must take for the next six to eight months due to the DVT in his left leg that has traveled to his groin. If it enters his heart or brain, he could have a stroke, a heart attack, or die.

Barb says she predicted that would be the result of the ultrasound, which lets her regurgitate her contention that she should have gone to medical school rather than get pregnant with Claire. She blames her first husband for both. All their life roads and events lead back to Barb and her past.

Alicia greets the news with silence. An hour later, she informs Gary that her SUV won't start and Barb needs to go to the grocery store. For the second time, he jump-starts her car and, this time, moves it inside their garage, hoping it will start the next time.

Gary walks Jack down the snow-covered street to get away from them. While they walk, he tells the dog, "Not a word of support from either of them. You gave me this DVT, and your fucking lazy but supposedly *independent* owner still won't walk you. This thing could kill me. I can't wait for you two idiots to never darken our door again."

Jack growls at him once as if he understands, then walks on.

When they finish the walk, Barb tells him, "Alicia's health has taken a turn for the worse. I almost took her to the nearest hospital this morning. She was holding onto the furniture while she walked. The weakness makes her a fall risk. I won't be long at the store. Just watch her until I return."

"Then maybe she needs to go home early. Be closer to her doctors in case she needs them. God forbid something happens to her here."

Barb makes a face. "I'm a nurse, and she has no supportive family. I can't send her home alone if she can't fend for herself. I won't be long."

While Barb shops, Alicia comes out of the guest bedroom, hair wrapped in a towel after her shower, and helps herself to food in their fridge. She shows no signs of fatigue or incapacitation.

"You seem to be getting around fine," Gary says. "What's your deal?"

Alicia smiles at him like the Mona Lisa. "It comes and goes. What do you mean by my *deal*?"

His eyes narrow. "You *know* what I mean."

She meets his gaze. "I'm friends with your wife, and she invited me here. Let me ask you this: which animal in the animal kingdom do you think is most like you?"

He stares at her, perplexed. "What? Why are you *really* here? You're a patient at the hospital where she works. As to your strange question, I guess I would choose the lion."

She shakes her head, unwraps the towel from her head, and brushes her hair. "That's not how I see you at all."

He laughs. The chutzpah on her is amazing. "Not that you know me, but which animal would you choose for me?"

The smile again. "Nope, I keep that to myself." She chose an ostrich for Gary days ago because he knows so little about his own wife, choosing to bury his head in the sand, but she will never tell him that. He will have to learn that on his own, probably the hard way.

"I have an animal in mind for you," he says. "The little fish that attach themselves to sharks. That's you."

Alicia nods. "Okay, they're called remoras. They hitch rides on sharks, they eat food that escapes the sharks' mouths, and they eat shark shit. I bet you didn't know they are not bloodsuckers and cause no pain to their host. They can also attach to sea turtles and sting rays."

He rolls his eyes because he should have said leech. His next word is void of emotion. "Whatever."

"I'm sorry you don't like me. I will be out of your hair soon. One way or the other."

Gary thinks to himself: *If only I could believe that.*

The garage door rumbles up, and before he says another word, he walks to the kitchen/garage door and helps Barb bring in groceries. When he hears Alicia shut the door to the guest room, he whispers: "She took a shower while you were gone and made herself a sandwich. There was no chair walking or holding onto walls. If she can do all that, she's fine to go home. I don't know what her game is, but she's playing one, and it's on you."

She scoffs. "You don't believe me? I've been a nurse for thirty years. She was in bad shape this morning. You just don't like her. You never like any of my friends."

"First off, she's a patient, not a friend, and you should damn well know that. It's almost the New Year. She needs to go home before something bad happens."

"How can you be so cruel? She has no family to help her."

He takes a deep breath. "I'm telling you, she has an ulterior motive for being here."

The rest of the evening, Alicia holds onto objects while she walks. She avoids Gary's eyes but plays the sympathy card with Barb, who takes her vitals and declares if she's not better by morning she will drive her to the local ER. Without a word, Gary takes his plate into the kitchen and retreats to the study.

The next day, Barb drives Alicia to the nearest ER for labs, observation, and monitoring. They find nothing to keep her. She was mildly dehydrated, and we picked her up that evening with prescriptions for Hydrocodone and Zofran as she told the hospitalist she'd been nauseous. Gary overhears Barb discussing her meds with her and learns she's on anti-depressants, anti-anxiety meds, hormone replacement therapies, and anti-inflammatories. She should not be ingesting or smoking pot.

Alicia is tearful and continues to chairwalk, telling Barb she's too weak to drive home the next day. When Barb looks the other way, she flashes a grin at him. That night, Barb and Gary continue to argue over whether Alicia is safe to return home. They get loud, and Gary wonders if Alicia can hear them.

In the morning, Alicia says she can barely stand and reports having a cluster headache. She's crying and talking about wanting to be dead, so we bring her back to the ER, where more tests are run, and again, nothing wrong is found. An MRI reveals the aneurysm has grown to 3.6. The hospitalist tells her to make an appointment with her PCP and suggests her psychiatrist review her meds.

Barb allows her to stay until Sunday night, the day before they are due to return to work. Alicia cries and whines that she's not ready to be alone, but they convince her she'll be alone in their house while they work.

Gary must jump Alicia's SUV a final time. Barb doesn't want her to drive home in her condition, so Barb takes Alicia and Jack in her fire-red Camaro while Gary follows in her SUV. They fill her prescriptions along the way and buy food and other supplies for her.

Alicia has a two-story house next to a creek somewhere in the vicinity of Belleville, Illinois. The hardwood floors are in the process of being installed. There is next to nothing on the walls, and Gary wonders how long she's lived there. Jack runs to the fenced backyard and pees for a long time.

On the drive home in the Camaro, Gary says, "What a nightmare. Jumping her damn car every time, walking her fucking dog." He makes a face and sniffs the air. "What is that awful smell?"

Barb groans. "I think Jack had an accident in the back seat. Alicia wasn't so bad. We did a nice thing for someone during the holidays who doesn't have family or much money."

Gary scoffs. "She told you she didn't have the copay for her meds, so you paid them, right? She has over fifty bucks in her glove compartment and a switchblade. What all did you treat her to?"

Barb waves a hand in the air as if to dismiss him. "You rooted around in her car?"

"Damn straight."

Minutes pass in silence. "The stay was my treat—a massage, facial, mani-pedi, and we had our eyelashes done. I gave her some money for her electric bill, which was in arrears. If I were single and lived alone, I may keep a knife in my car as well. Let me feel good about this right now. Don't ruin it for me, like everything else. We can afford it."

Three nights later, Gary wakes Barb complaining of pain, fever, and a swollen arm that feels hot and hard. His blood pressure tanks so severely that Barb drives him to the ER, where he's found to be in septic shock and admitted for a course of IV antibiotics. He's so fatigued that, at times, he can't lug his IV pole to the bathroom and wets himself or urinates in the trash can.

Barb visits him the first night, but as his stay lengthens, she's more of a no-show. She tells him she must go home after work to let out the dogs, but she doesn't return. He's too focused on his own health to wonder why she hasn't visited more. A week into his stay, as the doctor continues to struggle to find the right combination of antibiotics to knock out the sepsis, it looks like he may need surgery on his arm to remove the remaining drug-resistant infection. The night he learns this, his cell rings, and it's a frantic, distraught Barb.

"You've got to come home right now and help me!"

A flabbergasted Gary says, "I'm on three IV antibiotics, I can barely get out of bed to pee, and the doc told me he plans to operate on my arm in the morning to remove a stubborn pocket of infection. If you'd ever visit, you'd know this." He pauses during the awkward silence to process what she said. "Help you with what?"

A long pause on the line makes Gary think she's hung up. Then she whispers in a frightened voice, "Alicia."

He watches his blood pressure rise on the monitor at the mention of the name. "You let her back in our house while I've been hospitalized?"

"I did."

"Without telling me?"

"I knew you'd say no."

"So, you let her have the run of our house while you're at work?"

"No. The first day, I called in, and my asshole boss said I had to come in because I've taken too many days off, so I quit."

He laughs into the cell. "You quit your job without talking to me. For Alicia?"

The uncomfortable silence grows until Barb makes it worse. "You have got to come home and get her out of here."

"You're kidding, right?"

"No."

"I can't believe this. That you let her back in and that you want me to come home. Have you forgotten how difficult it was to get her to leave the first time?"

She sighs into the phone but says nothing.

His head spins from the insanity of this conversation with his wife. "Why do *you* want her gone now?"

"She made more pot brownies, climbed into bed with me, and broke our bed, and she drew a pentagram on the wall over the bed with candlewax. She's scaring me. I heard her rooting around in the basement today. I went down there, and I think she was trying to pry open your gun case. Hell, I'm so paranoid from the pot I'm not sure what's real and what isn't."

He runs a hand through his dirty hair. "I'm beginning to think there was more than marijuana in those brownies. Call the cops. They will escort her out. File a restraining order if you need to, but I can't help you from here."

Before she hangs up, she says, "You're no fucking help."

Later that night, their elderly neighbor Susan across the street calls Gary on his cell to say Barb knocked on her door a half hour ago, half naked and babbling, wanting her help with something at home but she wouldn't say what.

"She was upset and sounded … wild. I offered to return to your house with her and stay with her if she wanted me to, but she never said what she needed help with. Then she walked to Bob and Jill's house and knocked on their door, but no one answered. Then I saw her go back home. I know she'd been drinking. She walked through the snow barefoot."

Susan asks Gary how he's doing, and he briefly recaps he will need to be in the hospital for several more days.

"Thanks for offering to help her, Susan. I think I know what's going on." He lets it go at that, knowing elderly Susan will at least keep an eye on the home. Alicia's SUV is in their garage, and he doesn't want to ask Susan if she's seen anyone else in their home.

Two days later, Barb visits Gary the day after his surgery and simply says she was able to convince Alicia to go home. She provides no details and denies calling the police.

His surgery generally went well, and when he returned home, there was no evidence that candlewax was ever on the walls, but the sideboard of their bed was cracked, so he screwed it back together before it cracked all the way.

Barb remains mum about the second Alicia visit. Gary believes that Barb quit her job once Alicia threatened to blow the whistle to Barb's boss about being invited to spend a week in their home. God knows what allegation Alicia had invented to make Barb's life miserable, but he's certain she had one. He tries to think of possible motives Alicia may have had for doing what she did. He can only think Alicia wanted to drive a wedge between him and Barb, based on how she interacted with him that week, but what was the purpose? For money? To somehow worm her way into their home on a permanent basis? To replace him? It all sounds crazy, but he can't think of another reason.

The entire time is so bizarre it appears surreal.

Three months after his return from the hospital, Barb receives a letter with no return address. It's from Alicia's best friend (according to Barb), and the entire letter is a cutting rebuke of Barb for how badly she treated Alicia, and the letter-writer describes Barb as a borderline personality.

Gary thinks *the diagnosis applies to all three of you.*

Barb's drinking increases, and she takes her time finding another job, this time at a nursing home rather than a hospital, since she's burned her bridges in every nearby hospital.

Her lone comment to him about Alicia months later is that she wasn't *all that bad.*

The Bomb Explodes

"It takes two to make a union, but only one to break it."

Gary

For the next six months, Barb drinks and bemoans her fate to anyone who listens. She flits from various nursing home jobs, quitting them because she says her boss is an idiot, or he has no clue how to run the facility, or she's left alone to care for over fifty residents. She quit her most recent job the day before she was to be off probation after she told Gary she had a *run-in* with a second-shift security guard. The next day, Gary finds two empty pint vodka bottles in her car. He attends Al-Anon meetings and tries to convince her to attend AA meetings or consider an intensive outpatient program, but she refuses and says he doesn't love her. One afternoon, she gets out of bed and contacts her shrink's office to tell him she just swallowed all her meds. The office calls for an ambulance, and when the crew arrives, Barb is doing an Anne Frank in their bedroom closet, hiding while she screams at Gary not to answer the door. The short inpatient stay achieved nothing other than stabilizing her body for a few days, and she refused to continue as an outpatient.

When home, she sleeps, verbally jousts with Gary and her "ungrateful" kids, drinks, and loses her cell phone daily. Gary found it in the freezer, in the trashcan, the shower, on top of her car, and in the backyard. They've had to replace her lost phone three times. She throws out bizarre ideas to improve the house and curses Gary when he refuses to consider installing a below-ground pool that would take up their entire backyard. She also argues with Gary to give a portion of his inheritance to her sons so they can make down payments on starter houses. He refuses.

One afternoon, he receives a call from a cop at the local police station telling him his wife is in jail for driving under the influence of Ambien and alcohol, that she also drove over a mailbox and damaged the underside of her car to the extent it's not drivable. Gary asks when he can pick her up and is told she is still under the influence. Gary picks her up the next morning, and Barb is livid that she never received an offer of *professional courtesy* from the cop (do nurses and cops even have reciprocal professional courtesy, he wonders?) and that Gary did not pick her up the night before. She (a person who never has a good word to say about cops) expected the officer to let her go with a warning because she's an RN. They later meet with an expensive attorney to represent her, who says the good news is she was not legally intoxicated per the breathalyzer. Gary deals with the four-thousand-dollar repair of her car and pays to replace the neighbor's destroyed mailbox. They must pay a hefty fine and the legal fees. Barb informs him that she no longer wants to drive her repaired car because of the "negative memories," so they buy her a new car while Gary drives her repaired one.

During one of their verbal arguments over his inheritance, he grabs his keys to leave and lets her cool down once she starts repeating the same points ad nauseum be-cause he knows from experience there is no point to continue arguing with her when she's in this state. Barb curses him and says she wishes he would die. She pushes him from behind while he descends the steps from the kitchen to the garage. He doesn't fall headlong onto the hood of his car because he catches the railing.

He knows that when things get physical in a marriage, they only get worse. She's recently thrown a ceramic cup at his head, which broke against the wall, and recently, she's been bringing a steak knife to bed with her and hiding it under her pillow. He asked her about it, and she amazingly had nothing to say. She's made superficial cuts to her arms off and on but can't fathom why she needs a knife in their bedroom unless it's meant for him.

He meets with a divorce attorney and decides to file after the pushing incident. He fills out an order for protection, and a judge signs it. It's late in the day and Gary's prepared to spend the night in a hotel if need be. He brought the clothes on his back and his wallet. The police go to their home to serve the order. Gary is prepared to learn that Barb refused to open the door, but to his surprise, he receives a call that she agrees to leave. Per the order, she cannot come within 500 feet of him. He imagines her being belligerent with the two cops but never learns how the scene played out. He returns home and starts packing her belongings in boxes. She calls his cell constantly, screaming and cursing at him, wishing he would "just die." He stops answering. She texts him on his computer with foul, hate-filled rhetoric until he blocks her ability to do so.

He doesn't block her access to their credit cards and soon finds she's removed thirteen of the fifteen grand in their joint account before he closes it out and opens a new one in his name only. He also learns she had two credit cards unknown to him in her name only that she's been using to help her ne'er-do-well adult children and using money from their joint account to pay those bills. Their attorneys talk, and they schedule agreed-upon times for her to pick up her boxed clothes and other items. She sends her two sons in her place to transport her belongings, along with a list of things she wants from the house.

They've both been divorced once already, so they know how horrible the process can be. Gary finds he doesn't miss Barb at all. In fact, he feels relief he no longer must accept her frequent verbal harassment and abuse, staying up all hours of the night listening to the never-ending sob stories about how badly her first husband treated her over twenty years ago and how all her bosses were stupid and that she always knew more than them. No more money games from her, no more constant demands for money for her kids. No more trips with her to inpatient psych units; no longer must he listen to her rant about how she will eventually kill herself, maybe after she kills her first ex-husband. When he tells his close friends, all are supportive, and a few seem relieved, given Barb's bizarre behaviors over the years that have included her insisting they not attend gatherings of his friends because she suddenly became sick to her stomach or was in one of her dark moods about something her ungrateful kids supposedly said or did. He felt he'd abandoned his friends to appease Barb's over-developed need for attention.

Barb occasionally sends him a letter, wanting them to try again, promising she will be better, but inevitably, the note devolves into the same, tired protestations from her that she is right about everything and how badly he and the world have treated her.

He agrees to allow her to have their older dog, the one she is closest to, while he keeps the younger one. Gary offers to allow the dogs to occasionally see and play with each other, but Barb nixes the idea, and it never happens.

Gary feels like a huge weight has been lifted from his shoulders, and a blissful calm returns to his house. In time, he removes every picture of Barb from the house and paints over every too-bright, too-colorful room that she chose, including pink, red, green, and orange. He deletes the names and numbers of Barb's children from his phone. Eventually, the shell-shocked feeling ingrained in him since he met Barb recedes to a dull, occasional memory. He finalizes plans to retire early and pursue his hobbies of hunting, fishing, and traveling with his friends. He takes a break from women for two years and tells himself all he needs is an occasional companion with whom to take to restaurants and the occasional movie. Unlike Barb, he doesn't feel the constant need to be in a relationship and decides to never marry again.

The Hunter Cornered in the Jungle

"It's only fair, after what I gave up for you."

Jean

After Alicia returns home from the failed long game that involved Barb and Gary, she opens a text from her mother with an attachment. It's a grainy photograph of a woman in a floppy hat at nighttime. She remembers her score at the casino from the hairy poker player.

Below the pic, Jean has typed: "Billie Lee's memory is returning about that night. You need to visit me today and bring what I asked for. We will talk about future payments."

Alicia curses aloud, which wakes Jack. She looks up the number for the casino at the other end of the state, calls, and asks to be connected to the concierge desk. She asks for Billie Lee and lies that she's her cousin and that it's an urgent family matter. The man on the other end says, "I'm sorry, but Billie no longer works here, and we don't give out former employee's phone numbers. Have a blessed day!"

The curses continue while she talks to herself. She roots in the hidey-hole under the floorboard. She removes a dusty bag and counts out $500 from the twenties.

The SUV won't start so she takes a bus to the Terrace Arms. The elevator remains broken, and the same dubious cast of drug dealers hang out like statues on the darkened landings.

She knocks on the door since the bell doesn't work, either.

Jean feigns surprise when she opens the door. "Should've called first. You finally come to your senses?"

Alicia walks past Jean and sees Missy and Ty playing a video game on the sofa.

She grins. "You two losers have been in that same position ever since Christmas?"

"Pretty much," Ty says, without a care in the world.

Neither step-kid works or attends school. They, like Jean, are on Medicare and Medicaid for depression, anxiety, and nebulous health issues. They receive government money, which Jean controls. They play video games, read comic books, and watch television. Both are pasty white and rarely venture outside. Alicia suspects Missy is anorexic and another abuse survivor. Ty likes to bully her every chance he gets. Alicia is certain that neither possesses her street smarts nor even Jean's.

"We're not talking about this in the kitchen, where those little shits can hear," Alicia whispers to her mother.

She follows Jean into her bedroom and closes the door.

"I can't believe you want to blackmail your own daughter, especially after what happened to me."

Jean places her ashtray on the nightstand and flicks her ashes into the bowl. She smiles at her. "Nothing in this world is free or fair. Those two little insects out there wasting their lives on my sofa? I get half of their checks, which help pay the rent, utilities, and various household sundries. What's gonna happen to them when I'm gone? Don't know. They don't seem to care about it, neither. They choose to live in the most dull-looking moments. That isn't my concern. The world sucks. Life sucks. You think you're the only incest survivor on the planet? I was kicked out of the house when I was fourteen after my dad raped and impregnated me."

This is the first time Alicia's heard this. "What became of the kid?"

"Turn around."

Alicia turns and sees herself in the full-length mirror on the door.

"You're looking at her."

Alicia seems stunned by this but says nothing.

Jean moves closer to her. "A Catholic women's shelter took me in. I wanted to abort you, but if I did, I couldn't stay there. I tried to kill myself a couple of times while I carried you, but each time someone stopped me."

"I don't believe you."

She shows Alicia the old scars on her left wrist. "This, and some overdoses."

The wry smile returns. "Why do you think there are no pictures of you until you were four? The nuns raised you when you were an infant, then a foster home. Until I was nineteen. By then, I'd given up my dream of an honorable, good-paying profession and decided you were the one unique thing I had. Looking back, part of that may have been the nuns brainwashing me. I was living with a foster family who agreed to let me help care for you if I met certain state criteria."

Alicia crosses her arms. "Why'd the state give custody of me to you with your history and all the suicide attempts?"

She crushes a butt in the ashtray. "They didn't at first. My foster parents were your actual guardians for the first few years, but they were getting older, and the responsibility was too much for them. I can't blame them for wanting a break from you in their golden years. If not for them, you wouldn't be here, and we wouldn't know each other."

The news she was a product of rape almost makes her forget the reason for her visit. "Now, you want to extort money from me?"

"Blackmail, extort. Call it an act of charity or giving a little something back to the woman who gave birth to you; call it whatever you want. You owe me."

"If I give you the money, what's to stop you from demanding more?"

Jean smiles again. "Not a damn thing, sugar, unless you cotton to the idea of going back to jail. You need to trust your mama and her judgment."

Alicia laughs. "Why would I start now?"

She pulls out another cigarette. "I found a better apartment in a nicer neighborhood. Three bedrooms so the losers on the sofa can finally get their own rooms. Rent is three hundred more, but—"

"I don't need or want the details. Your friend Billie Lee doesn't work at the casino anymore."

Jean laughs. "Your point? We're still friends, and she's a phone call away."

Alicia steps closer to her mother. "How about I … terminate you instead?"

"Like to see you try. Far tougher than you have tried." Jean reveals the tip of a switchblade from a sweater pocket.

Alicia glares at Jean and reaches into her jeans pocket. "You have no idea what I sacrificed to get this money."

"Rolling marks and making a living on your knees or back? Shit, you're living my life thirty years ago. If you've got half a brain, you squirreled away a chunk of that and can afford to pay a little tax on it. Consider me the IRS when it comes to your undeclared income."

She hands over the wad, and Jean counts it twice.

"Thanks. I remember next Thursday is your birthday. C'mon over for dinner to celebrate at six. No reason we can't be civil to each other. We're in business together!"

Alicia turns to leave. "No, thanks."

"Better rethink that answer. I need a twelve-hundred-dollar deposit for the apartment the day after your birthday. Cash. Do that, and your monthly tax remains at five hundred, for now. We'll discuss what you're doing wrong in your *enterprises,* and I can give you pointers on ways to improve your bottom line and which fences are safe and pay the most."

There's a knock on the bedroom door.

Alicia spins around and whispers in Jean's ear. "Remember this: I've acquired other items besides spare cash. Loud things with triggers." Alicia smirks at Jean.

Jean doesn't back down. "Be here at six, grasshopper."

Alicia throws open the door and walks past a surprised Ty, who didn't hear her arrive. She hears Ty ask Jean if they're moving this month. The bitch Jean has been planning this for months.

On her way out, Alicia hands Missy a business card for a local sliding-scale therapist. "You want to talk to someone about what you went through; they can help."

She drives halfway across the state to pawn three watches, two handguns, and a man's wedding ring, all acquired last year. Her policy is to hold onto non-cash items for at least a year before selling them in case there's still heat on them.

In a show of defiance, she returns to Jean's intentionally late on Thursday at 6:30 pm.

"Your watch broke?"

"Bus ran late."

Jean scoffs. "Why don't you just put a new battery in that damn car?"

"It comes in handy the way it is."

Jean points to an open box on the kitchen table. "Happy birthday."

Alicia removes her coat and pulls up a kitchen chair next to Ty and Missy, who've already started to eat the birthday dinner—a 30-pack Crave Case of cheeseburger sliders from White Castle, fries, chicken rings, and chocolate and strawberry shakes. They throw empty boxes at each other until Alicia shouts, "Stop, or I will knock the shit out of you!"

They acquiesce to the Alpha female.

"Wow, I see you went all out for my goddamn birthday."

"I remember this was your favorite food."

Alicia chooses a strawberry shake that's now runny. "When I was ten."

Ty laughs until Alicia scowls at him.

"They couldn't wait any longer. The smell was driving them crazy. Big surprise," Jean says.

Alicia squirts a packet of ketchup on a small, greasy, cold, onion-filled slider. "Does anybody know which baby shark cannibalizes each other in the womb?"

Jean rolls her eyes. "This is hardly dinner talk. Again."

"The great white is the only shark I know by name," Missy guesses.

Alicia takes a bite and shakes her head. "It's the sand shark. The females have two uteruses and many eggs. They become impregnated by multiple male sharks. The largest embryo will eat all the smaller ones except one. It's part of a struggle for paternity in utero, where babies of different fathers compete to be born. Sand sharks have two babies that are killers before they're even born. That's so cool it's stone cold."

Ty belches, and Alicia slaps the back of his head.

"Where do you learn this stuff?" Missy asks, suddenly interested.

"Shark week. Fascinating, isn't it?"

"Why do you insist on talking this way?" Jean asks.

"It comes rushing back whenever I visit you."

"Well, I don't like it. Not one bit. Don't blame me for your sick thoughts."

Alicia glances at Ty and Missy. "You two need to learn that nature is harsh and unforgiving, whether animal or people, in water or on land, and that sometimes you don't even get a chance to live, much less make something of yourself in this world. Twenty-five species of sharks must swim constantly, or they will die. Do you know why?"

Missy stops chewing to stare at her.

"They lack a swim bladder and it's how they obtain oxygen from the water. You plan to sit on that sofa playing video games until your lives go by?"

Neither answer. Ty looks away while Missy looks to the floor.

"I'd rather see you on the streets. Or outside walking or playing sports. Your asses get wider each time I see you. Live on that sofa, and you will die."

Jean rolls her eyes. "Ty and Missy, throw your empties in the trash and go watch television."

Alicia turns to Jean once they leave. "So, what do you think you can teach me about what I do that I don't already know?"

Jean lights up a cigarette and sips her tea. She reaches out a hand. "Business first."

She counts the stack of twelve hundred-dollar bills. "Some of these are sequential. You must have visited a pawn shop." She looks at her daughter, waiting for a response.

Alicia nods.

"You go to Ardi's or Tiny's pawn store?"

"Neither. I wait a year in case the goods have been reported and are possibly on lists at pawn stores. Then I drive across the state." She doesn't mention that she resells the drugs on the street to dealers she knows, which is how she gets the roofies.

Jean takes a drag. "That's smart in one way and dumb in another. I get not wanting to shit where you eat, but you burn gas and waste half a day. That's time you could be planning and doing the next job.

"You ever get caught by a mark or a hotel, not counting the casino video?"

"I don't do this full-time. I do it when I need extra money. I can't afford to pay you every month."

"Your illness ever get in the way?"

She lies. "Nope."

"When you find a mark, like the guy in the casino, do you sleep with them?"

Alicia pulls away and crosses her arms. "Why do you need to know that?"

Jean scoffs. "You're right. It's a dumb question that you just answered. You gotta wait until they fall asleep to roll them anyway, so my question is answered again. Just wanted to know how far you're willing to go, is all. I assume you have protection or insist they wear a condom."

Alicia doesn't answer.

"You have a current partner or use a convincer?"

She denies knowing what the word means.

"A convincer is a shill that draws other potential suckers into a con. Someone who can demonstrate the con game is beatable."

She shakes her head and thinks: Jean's way too nosy, so she will only know what I want her to hear.

"So, you don't do many street hustles like three card Monty, sell fake jewelry as the real deal, relationship scams, check fraud, or sell phony sports or concert tickets?"

She laughs. "Three-card Monty? Really, it's the 2020's, Jean."

"Okay, what about phishing, computer hacking, or bitcoin fraud? It's still not that hard to steal certain people's identities, especially the old or computer illiterate."

She shakes her head. "Who are you? You throw out all these con artist terms. You ever do these things?"

Jean grinds out a cigarette. "In my younger days. A woman does what she needs to do to survive in this world. "What about sex work? You know … being the voice on phone sex lines? Little effort and not much cost. Find the right clientele, it can be profitable. I'd do that myself right now if my voice weren't so old and gravelly. You have a sexy, deep voice. Men like that."

Alicia grimaces. "I avoid anything that involves me using my own money to set up a mark."

"Yes, I forgot you are a millennial. So, you're limited to enticing marks with that curvy bod and rolling them? Ever put someone on the send, or are you just a peanut grifter?"

Alicia fishes out her own cigarette.

"The long cons are the Holy Grail versus very small, short cons, and they're hard to come by.

"You met 'Savannah.' I was her confederate. She used me to help focus on a rich old woman. One who lives alone and is on the outs with her family and vice versa. We weaseled our way into being her caregivers and nearly gained access to her savings account."

"Yes, your former partner in crime told me about that one. The mark and the son ruined your plan. That could have been a righteous score if the son was out of the picture or if you'd drugged the old gal just enough to take the edge off and prepared her better with the exact words for her to say. A half day of practice with you acting as the bank manager would have helped seal the deal." Jean shakes her head. "How far are you willing to go when you put someone on the send? I say, whatever it takes."

She stares back at this new side of Jean. "I believe that of you."

Alicia never thought about drugging little old Myrtle before they went to the bank. *Maybe Jean can be of some help, after all.*

"*That* might have helped lighten her up when she went to the bank, but she was already on a lot of meds."

"You didn't hear me? *Whatever* it takes."

Alicia looks at her watch. "The last bus is due in ten minutes."

Jean takes the hint. "One last question. When you take a mark to his hotel room, do you drug them or wait for them to go to sleep after the booze and sex?"

She grabs her coat. She doesn't need to know how I roll. "They're not always men. It depends on my assessment of each one and how big a threat they pose."

Jean smirks while she tries to read her daughter's face. "Hmm. You sound like part of you wants to get pinched. I'd drug them all to make sure. You don't want any surprises at a time like that. Hotel casinos also have far too many video cameras to record people coming and going. Cheaper hotels are better. I'd avoid chronic gamblers if I were you. To be safe. Most are paranoid, streetwise, and desperate."

Jean calls to her on her way out. "There's a conference at the Ritz coming up in a few weeks for business managers. I used to fleece certain events there when I was your age and a friend of mine still works there as a maid. I will talk with her and see what it takes for her to open some doors for us. You might want to case the layout and the exits.

"And get a new car battery. It's your getaway vehicle. At some point, you will invariably need to depend on it." She shakes her head and makes a clucking sound, "Taking the bus, for God's sake."

The next morning, Alicia gets her SUV serviced and a new battery installed.

All in the Family?

"P.T. Barnum was right about suckers."

Nick

He follows at a discreet distance and watches her take a seat at the bar. He waits until she's about to finish her first drink before he walks up and catches the bartender's eye. He orders a shot of Jack and a beer for himself and smiles at Alicia before he tells the bartender to put her next martini on his tab.

She discreetly notices his ass and long hair. Dressed in black, his blue-green eyes smile at her again. He seems the embodiment of every man who never looked twice at her and was too good for her in the past. Something stirs in her. Now he's staring at her, and she feels a warm glow wash over her.

She raises her glass to him. "Thanks."

"You're welcome."

He picks up his drinks, and as he turns to go back to his table, she says, "Going back to sit with your girlfriend?"

"I don't have one."

"Table or girlfriend?"

"Neither."

"Sit here."

The smile again. "Okay, thanks."

No polite chit-chat follows. No discussion of jobs, families, or hobbies. They listen in silence to the band and order another round until she says, "You're not gay, are you? Why no girlfriend?"

"Either I get bored or happen upon someone else. Not looking to settle down. Just looking for a good time."

She faces him. He has a panther tattoo on his right arm and a clock without hands on his left wrist. "I like your ink." Her next words sound almost collegial. "Where'd you do your time?"

Little does she know the only prisons he's ever seen are on television. An eyebrow raises, and their eyes lock. "How do you know prison tattoos?"

"Firsthand knowledge. Why don't we get out of here and have a … *good time*."

He drains his beer and follows her.

She rents a room at the motel across the street. She's heavier than other women he's dated, but he stays in character. Thirty minutes of frenzied sex later, she asks him what he learned in the joint.

He answers right away. "Never to go back. You?"

"There's that, but I also learned cons."

"That's what they pinched me for."

She traces a fingernail along a pronounced vein in his arm. "Really?

The excitement in their voices builds while they talk about specific cons.

She dresses, and before she leaves, he says, "You wanna do this again? I work weekends at *The Corner Bar*. We close at one. Look me up."

She leaves without a word.

He worries he's lost her.

The green Monte Carlo idles at midnight across the street from a local shopping center as Alicia walks toward it. The driver instructs her to walk into the alley near the Dumpster, which she does without breaking stride or looking at the car. A minute later the man who'd rode shotgun opens a service entrance of the establishment next to the Dumpster. Mateo's a slightly framed Puerto Rican in a wife-beater t-shirt and rolled-up jeans that are too long for him.

"What you got for me this time, Booster?"

She always liked his nickname for her and hands over Mr. G's Glock. "Let's start with this."

He inspects it under the glow of the rear entry light, then says, "You got the second cartridge and the box of hollow points that match the ones in the gun?"

She shakes her head. "What you see is what you get, Mateo, if the price is right."

He holds up a hundred-dollar bill.

She knows it's a fair deal, but she frowns. "A pawn shop would double that."

Mateo smirks. "Good luck with the serial number filed off. A legit dealer would probably report you to the po-po."

Reluctantly, she nods and takes the Benjamin.

He quickly scans the alleyway and sees no movement. "Anything else?"

She produces Mr. G's Rolex.

He whistles and inspects it closely. "It's a nice one. For this style, I can go all the way up to a grand. You know a pawn shop would give you twice that, so this one must be hot and local, am I right? Just so I know what I'm buying and where I can move it."

She smiles. She remembers the address on Mr. G's driver's license and nods her head. "We have been doing business for how long now?"

He gives her the grand.

"That it?" Mateo asks, again scanning the alley.

She holds up the vial she stole from Mr. G and says, "Can I trade this coke for Fentanyl?"

"You don't wanna mix the two?"

"Nope. Whatever I can get for the vial."

He frowns for a moment. "Taking a walk on the wild side, eh? Sounds like uncharted territory for you. Stay here." He walks through the back door of the business establishment and returns in ten minutes with a small baggie.

"Need more roofies, Booster?" Mateo asks, patting his pocket.

Alicia shakes her head as she turns around to leave the alley. "Thanks. See you again, hopefully soon."

Four days later, Alicia drives to *The Corner Bar* and parks a block away. She enters fifteen minutes before it closes. Her head feels like a band is playing discordant notes from bagpipes and accordions while her vision grows blurry. She sits on a stool and a muscular, long-haired bartender dressed in black winks and places her usual martini in front of her. He then nods to a waiter and shakes the old man at the far end of the bar.

"Hey, Milton! Wake up. Your Uber will be here in five minutes." Tommy here will walk you out and sit with you on the bench till it arrives. Time to go!"

The old man startles awake. "One more for the road, Nicky-me-boy?"

The man shakes his head as Milton stares at the dangling gold cross earring on Nick's left lobe. He points his hand toward the door. "Tommy."

"See you tomorrow, Nicky-me-boy."

Nick nods and tosses something metallic in a pot by the rows of liquors. "I'm sure. Bring your friend with you to get your car keys back, or don't drink so much."

After Nick closes out the bills of the remaining bar flies, he refills Alicia's glass. Tommy wipes down the last of the tables and prepares to leave. Nick turns off the neon sign and locks the front door after Tommy.

He closes out the register and crams the tips into the front of his tight jeans.

"You look like shit, babe. What's up?"

She drains the drink and stands to face him. "You. In a minute. In the back. Now."

He laughs. "Didn't know you were coming. Back room's filthy."

She removes her top as she walks by him. "So am I."

"How about we go to my place? I got something to run by you."

The blouse falls to the floor. "Fine. After. Get in here."

He barely makes it into the tiny back room when she throws him on the mattress. He unbuttons his shirt while she pulls at his cowboy boots. She struggles with the second one before she focuses on his belt buckle.

Afterward, he notices one boot is still on when he pulls up his underwear and pants before he walks into the dingy half-bath to throw water on his face. He notices the scratch marks on his back from her nails. It's two in the morning. He takes a deep breath and remembers to stay in character as he returns to her. He puts his shirt back on and combs his locks with his fingers.

"Something happened yesterday, babe? You came here with a real bug up your ass. Mom set you off somehow?"

She's dressed and ready to go. She grins. "What makes you say that?"

"What you were saying in bed. You were pissed at someone and seemed to take it out on me." He laughs. "I wasn't sure I was gonna still be in one piece when you were done."

"Hell, you might be right. Got some aspirin?"

He throws her the bottle. He grabs the keys and sets the alarm before they leave the bar. "Wanna grab some food at the diner? Got something to run by you."

They walk a few blocks and cross the street to enter the large, all-night diner named *Smilin' Sally's Truck Stop,* not far from the interstate. They grab a booth in the back, and an elderly lady shaped like a bowling pin slaps down two coffee cups on their checkercloth table. An unlit cigarette dangles from her thin lips as she offers two menus.

"Why are you working, Sally?" Nick says.

Her eyes barely open; the tiny slits look his way. "Another day in paradise. One waitress has hep C, 'nother ran off with one of her boyfriends, one called in, and the cook is getting the tips of his fingers sewn back on." She leans forward and whispers. "Stay away from the chili tonight."

Alicia orders a burger, fries, and a strawberry milkshake while Nick asks for the steak special rare and a double Jim Beam neat.

Sally looks at Alicia's messed hair and then at Nick. "Food'll be a while. I'll bring the drinks. Might want to rebutton your shirt there, Romeo." She walks toward the kitchen with a slow gait like a wobbly ten-pin.

He looks down and curses while he fixes his shirt. "You know that thing you brought up the last time?"

She nods while she lights up. After midnight, Sally lets select customers in the back booths near the can smoke one cigarette at their own risk.

He whispers. "I have the equipment to make the IDs and the solution we need. You still up for this?"

This is an easy sell. Anything that makes money without involving Jean is a good thing, especially since she put a temporary squeeze on me. "I'm in."

Sally drops off the drinks. She notices the fixed shirt and turns to Alicia, "He's a looker. I hope he found the right holes earlier."

She smiles and blows a smoke ring in the air. "Let's say he smooths over my edges."

Sally's lone response is, "Food will be twenty minutes if you're lucky. Drink up. I'm doing double duty."

When Sally sidles back toward the kitchen, Nick says, "We're going to use multiple phony IDs to open bank accounts at several local banks. Deposit and withdraw a few bucks every now and then so the accounts look legit. When that's in place, we need to obtain personal checks that have been written out and signed. No employer checks. The best are credit card payments, utility bills, or checks made out to family members. If you can make an educated guess about how much the mark may have in their account, even better. Do not get caught. When we have them, I will show you how to wash them. The rest is easy."

"The split?"

"Fifty-fifty, once I recover the cost of the equipment. The solution is cheap."

The food comes fifty minutes later after Nick has a buzz, and Alicia pours some of his fourth bourbon in her second milkshake. The aspirin helped some, but she drove home with a dull pain behind her eyes and a cluster headache.

She could do the easy thing and wait till nightfall to riffle through mailboxes and find outgoing checks, but instead, Alicia drives to case Barb and Gary's upper-middle-class neighborhood and the subdivision next to it. She parks in a quiet cul-de-sac and observes the traffic around the six homes in the morning, afternoon, and evenings, as well as street lighting and the habits of the postal carrier truck. Her tinted car windows provide adequate privacy. She walks around enough to remember the last names on the mailboxes and spots a security camera above one garage door and a doorbell cam at a second house. The backyards slope to common ground and beyond the woods is the other subdivision. She learns single elderly women appear to live in two homes, and one of them uses a walker; three homes have several school-age children whose friends visit and play in the backyards, while the fifth house contains a young, childless couple that lives next to Barb and Gary. Three homes have cleaning services and other deliveries. She writes this all in a notebook and learns what she can online about every household.

On a moonless night, she parks in the subdivision below and walks up the sidewalk at 2 a.m. wearing a head covering and nondescript clothes. There is no traffic in the cul-de-sac and no lights on inside any of the houses. The first two boxes are empty, but the next one has its flag up. She freezes when the front porch light winks on but realizes it's a motion sensor. It belongs to the woman with the walker, and the mailbox door creaks when she opens it. A neat stack of outgoing mail held together with a rubber band. Alicia takes it all and hardly breaks stride. The next three are empty, but the last two have today's mail still inside. She takes this and continues down the sidewalk. She removes a pocket flashlight, scans the mail, and pockets one envelope from all three boxes. She waits five minutes, turns around, and replaces the other mail back where it was, taking care to shield her face from the cameras. She calmly walks to her car while the rush of getting away with stealing flushes her skin. A police cruiser passes without incident, and she smiles. The headache returns, and her neck feels stiff. For a moment, her vision blurs. She tells herself other thieves wouldn't have bothered to return the rest of the mail.

At home, she lets Jack out and opens the stolen mail. The envelope from the woman with the walker is addressed to someone with the same last name and contains a personal check for $25 made out to Sean Jones. In the memo line are the words 'Happy birthday!" She reads the short letter attached that tells how happy she was to witness Sean's baseball game months ago and looks at a few pictures of a skinny young boy standing at home plate in various stages of swinging a bat at a baseball. The look on his face indicates he's afraid of the ball. She tosses the letter and pictures in her burn-pile trash.

Bingo. This one will work.

The second envelope is incoming, from the mailbox of the young, childless Indian couple. Alicia earlier learned that both are doctors at an area hospital. He works as a cardiologist while his wife is an anesthesiologist. She chose this because of the matching name on the return address label. Inside is a personal check from his father, a retired MD, for $3,000.

The legal-size envelope pilfered from Barb and Gary's mailbox is outgoing, addressed from Gary to a law firm in town. Enclosed is a check for $2,500, and in the memo box is written the word 'retainer.' Alicia looks up the lawyer online and learns that he's a divorce attorney.

Alicia grins and removes the check, seals the letter back in the envelope, and mails it the next day. She is happy to stir the pot further. She tells herself they never should have married.

She meets Nick three days later in his one-bedroom loft in the city after she's pilfered eight more checks that should work for them. The place is grungy except for the old Formica kitchen tabletop, which is pristine.

"You bring everything I asked?"

She removes two meatball sub sandwiches, a pint of Jack Daniels, and a box of Moon Pies from a backpack.

"How many viable checks did you get?"

She looks at him and frowns. "Viable? What the hell? You Mr. Wizard college-boy all of a sudden? I got eleven that look good, two I'm confident we can write in a larger amount."

He groans and reminds himself to stay in character. "It's just another word that means live. We need live checks."

She continues to stare.

"Let's see what you got, and I'll show you how to wash."

He sits down with his check stack and studies hers before nodding approval.

"Prepare to be amazed."

He takes a check and places it face down on the flat table surface before he rubs the back of it with a craft knife. "See what I'm doing? This helps remove indentations created by the pen when the check was written."

He places the check on a couple of paper towels and takes a cotton swab from a glass dispenser. "You gotta be sure you get every little speck of ink. Tellers are trained to look for irregularities. Some people write in large, flowing sweeps, which can run into the ink imprinted on the check. So, before I work on each check, I study it carefully to make sure I know where all the ink is before I start."

He washes his hands, rolls up his sleeves, and dips a swab in acetone. "Before, I tried to dip each check in a solution, but that caused a problem with drying. Some never looked dry afterward or looked warped, whether I used a hair dryer or pressed them between heavy books, so I finetuned the wash. The less liquid used, the more realistic the checks will look. Watch closely." He gently wipes the swab across key parts of the check until the pen ink disappears.

Alicia looks dumbfounded at the bill. The pay-to-the-order line is now blank, as is the amount of the check. He blows on it before placing it on a paper towel to let it fully air dry.

Nick grabs a sub and the pint. "Your turn. Pretty simple, eh? "Wash your hands before you start to avoid transfers or smudges. Either that or wear these gloves." He stands and pats his seat. "Each check must pass inspection by the tellers when we deposit them into our dummy accounts, so they have to look perfect."

He watches her repeat his motions and suggests she use a little less acetone on the swab, telling her she can always add more if needed. He finds she left a lower loop of an *f* on the bank logo of one check and has her wash that area again.

"Aside from that, yours look as good as mine," Nick says as he reaches for the second sub. "While we wait for them to dry, did you learn anything about an account holder that could give us a ballpark figure on what we can write in?"

She takes a swig from his pint and refers to her notebook.

"The Bank of America account, check number 3416, was originally made out for three grand and came from a family member who's a retired MD living in a multi-million-dollar home in San Francisco. It came here to a big house in a great neighborhood where the couple both work as doctors with high-paying positions."

Nick grins as he wipes marinara sauce from his square chin. He pushes the long hair away from his face and leans back on his stool. "Any comment written in the lower left *Memo* line? Any note that indicates what the money's for?"

She shakes her head.

"I love cherries." He closes his eyes and thinks. "Put $25,600 in your book. Write that amount in after the check dries. Make sure to get that money right after it's deposited cause a big fish like that will contact his bank and raise holy hell.

"Any other ones?

Alicia produces Gary's check for $2,500 and says, "We can make this out for five grand, easy."

"Then write in nine thousand."

She mentions a few other promising checks, and Nick decides the amounts she should write in. The proposed total of her eleven stolen and freshly washed checks comes to over 51K.

"Can I write in the amounts now?"

He looks at the table. "Nah. They're still drying."

She narrows her lids and winks at him. "Let's go in the other room then."

He reaches into his pocket and turns off the Dictaphone. "Works for me, babe."

Hotel California

"I brought her into this world; I can damn well take her out."

Jean.

The cell rings and rings on the nightstand until Nick silences it. Alicia rises minutes later to check the message.

Jean's voice was calm and controlled. "Where the fuck are you?"

Alicia dresses and slaps his naked ass. "Gotta roll."

He pulls on his black jeans and calls to her. "Write those checks for the amounts I said and deposit them in the dummy accounts today. I mean *today*."

She waves to him while she leaves his apartment.

On the drive to the hotel, she buys a breakfast burrito and coffee. She parks in the employee lot behind the hotel and places an office phone in her bag. Before she enters the back door, she dons the employee hotel jacket and the badge Jean had given her.

Esmerelda opens the locked hotel door for her and ushers her into a small room near one of the currently unoccupied conference rooms.

"You," she tells her, pointing to a small desk while she hands her sheets of paper. "Se rapido. Andale, andale!" The short, hefty Mexican with a round face pushes her inside.

They hear people talking around the corner, but no one sees Esmerelda walk Alicia the other way down the hall toward the main entrance and hurry her into a small room.

Alicia locks the door, removes the phone from her bag, and plugs it into the phone jack. She reviews the list of recent guest sign-ins and dials a number.

"Mr. Otis Anderson in room 758?" she says.

An uncertain older voice. "Yes."

"Good afternoon, Mr. Anderson. Welcome to *The Breakers*. This is Susan at the front desk, covering for Steven, who checked you in a little while ago. He's on break right now, and I ran the card you provided him for the room, but it didn't go through. Do you have a minute to verify the correct card number or provide another credit card?"

In the background, Alicia hears a woman asking Otis who's on the phone.

Otis tells Betty not to worry and that everything is okay. Then he raises his voice and admonishes Betty to sit down before she falls.

Alicia smiles. One of the conferences at the hotel this week focuses on Alzheimer's Disease and its impact on caregivers.

It sounds like the phone is placed on a table, followed by muffled voices, before a frazzled Mr. Anderson returns to the line. Betty shouts, and Otis tells her to shush for a minute.

"Okay, Susan. Are you ready?"

Alicia smiles. *You bet your ass I'm ready.* "Yes, sir, go ahead with your card information, please."

Otis rattles off the name and number of their card, the security code, and the expiration date.

Alicia [Susan] says, "That was it! The last number on the card was entered incorrectly. Thank you very much, Mr. Anderson. I hope you and your wife enjoy your stay at *The Breakers* and please let us know if you need anything."

Otis thanks her and tells her to have a nice day before he disconnects. Thankful marks are the best.

There's no answer in many rooms and the next five answered calls don't go nearly as well. These five guests say they will personally come down to the registration desk rather than provide credit card information over the phone. One woman grills Alicia [Susan] for her last name and her supervisor's name and expects to meet with her personally in the next ten minutes. Two other guests ask her to repeat the credit card information she supposedly has on file, which causes her to hang up.

This makes her uneasy until she remembers no one knows where she is other than Esmerelda. She could be calling from a block away, another city, or another country. The last call she makes strikes pay dirt when a middle-aged-sounding woman gives her card information without a second thought.

A rapping at the door startles her until she remembers it's the special knock—two soft taps followed by three loud knocks. She puts away her phone and the list before opening the door.

Jean holds up a bunch of keys and smiles. "How'd it go?"

"I got two for you." She hands over the credit card info. "What's with the keys? I thought Esmerelda refused to give them up."

"She did. Got them when her back was turned. She's on lunch break. She works floors eight and nine today, so don't go there. Be quick and get the keys back to me in forty minutes in the back parking lot. I'll figure it out from there." Jean grins. "I miss doing shit like this. This is fun!"

Alicia hurries through the third and fourth floors, using the pass key to unlock the doors where no one answers her knocks. She's able to pick up watches, assorted jewelry, blank checks, and money until she senses the need to get out of there after she passes a cleaning woman by the elevators who stares at her.

In the lobby, she passes Esmerelda's keys to Jean and walks to her SUV. "Meet up at your apartment."

Jean nods.

Alicia beats Jean to her apartment and engages Missy in a lengthy conversation while Ty watches a Rambo movie for the twentieth time.

Alicia sets the hook early, and it takes Missy fifteen minutes for the tears to stop.

She puts her hand on Missy's arm. "Is this what you want out of life? Do you like living like a second-class citizen? You don't have to be dependent on her or take beatings from Ty."

She sniffles and shakes her head, her face flushed with emotion as she reaches for a tissue. She finally looks up at her older half-sibling. "What can I do about it?"

Alicia smiles and says in a soothing voice. "First thing is … keep your ears open. Call me immediately if you overhear Jean speak of any plot against me, no matter how small or insignificant you may think it sounds."

More sniffling. "Why would she do that?"

"She and I are working together. The only thing … she's not a team player, and at some point, she will try to cut me loose and keep everything for herself. Work with me on this and I promise your life will be worlds better with me than if you remain under her thumb. Trust me on this. We will come out on top." She squeezes her hand once.

Missy dabs at her eyes with a tissue and doesn't respond when the front doorknob turns, and Jean returns.

Alicia talks faster and under her breath. "Pull yourself together. Act like nothing's different, but keep your ears open after I leave. Listen to her phone calls when you can. There's a lot more of this for you if you hear anything and work with me." She slips her a twenty-dollar bill and leaves Jean's bedroom quickly while Jean hangs up her coat.

Alicia meets Jean in the kitchen to allow Missy time to return to the living room. She takes a Coke from the fridge when Jean suggests they discuss things in her bedroom.

She hands Alicia a credit card. "This one's closer to you in age. What do you have for me?"

Alicia splits the cash, and they take turns choosing the watches and jewelry. She withholds the checks for her other scam. "Did Esmerelda get her keys back?"

Jean frowns and lights up a cigarette. "What do you care?"

Exasperated, Alicia shrugs. "You want to burn your bridges at the hotel? What if she gets canned and decides to spill the beans about you?"

"I couldn't find her. I left them with the concierge and told her I found them by the elevator."

Alicia thinks of the shitstorm Esmerelda will face from her boss because of her mom. "That's not cool. Make good use of that credit card because this is the last time we work together. I can't work with you if you're going to be this sloppy."

She blows a smoke ring at Alicia. She looks at her as if she's a stain on the rug. "Who died and made you boss? We're done when I say we're done. You forget about the casino tape so soon?"

"I gotta roll."

Jean turns in her direction. "I will call when I find the next opportunity."

Without looking back, she says, "Whatever." She fixes her eyes on Missy on her way out. A faint, inscrutable smile crosses her face while she sits on the couch. Perhaps an almost imperceptible nod in Alicia's way?

She stops at several stores wearing the wide-brimmed hat and fills up her SUV with purchases made with the stolen Visa card. She lets Jack out to do his business in the tiny backyard and she again cuts then burns the stolen credit card. She pours a glass of wine and watches a taped episode from this year's *Shark Week* in which a group of scientists capture and release Great White sharks to study their mating habits. She always roots for the sharks and laughs when the announcer says that no person has ever witnessed the mating of Great Whites. As it should be, she says to herself. Keep your secrets from the world.

When she drove home an hour earlier, she failed to see the nondescript Camry parked down the street. Nor did she see Nick hunkered down in the driver's seat with a baseball cap shoved down to cover his face.

Catch and Release

"Most scumbags will do anything to regain their freedom. The trick is choosing the right ones and using them to suit our needs."

Detective Ian Jameson

Nick watched his old man sell Encyclopedia Britannica door-to-door when he was six years old. From there, he remembers his dad selling Fuller Brushes and, later, sets of knives with exotic names from the trunk of his car. His mother's friends described his dad as a tall, handsome man with natural charms and charisma who carried himself well. At the end of each workday, Nick Senior brought home a six-pack and a cigar and, on Fridays, a racing form. Mom would usually have dinner ready for them within an hour of his arrival. Cube steaks, liver and onions, and pot roast were the most frequent dinner entrees, along with scalloped potatoes or green beans. Hamburger or Tuna Helper when money was tight, which was often the case. Violet, his mom, worked part-time at the nearby Catholic grade school as a secretary to the Monsignor.

When Nicky was fourteen, Nick took him to the racetrack for the first time. On the way, they stopped at a convenience store, and when he saw the young man at the cash register, his dad told him to *pay attention and learn*. He recalls every detail of what happened.

Dad grabs a pack of gum and acts like he's in a hurry while he puts down a twenty-dollar bill on the counter to pay for the ninety-cent purchase. His steely blue eyes smile at the clerk while he leans forward. He gets his change and says,

"You know what, sonny? I didn't want to break that twenty. If I give you a five-dollar-bill and five singles back, can you give me a ten?" His dad precedes to give the young clerk the five and four singles, and the clerk passes him the ten, but when the clerk says he only gave him nine dollars, he says, "I might as well take back the twenty. Here's another dollar, which makes ten, and here's another ten, so can I get back my twenty?" The harried young clerk does as he's told, and they walk slowly back to their car.

"What just happened, Nicky?"

He squints up at his dad and thinks about the exchanges. "I think you bought gum and made ten dollars."

His dad smiles down at him and hands him a stick of gum. "Good boy. You just witnessed your first short-range con game. This ten is for you to spend at the track however you want. If you want to make a bet on a horse with some of that money, I will do it for you."

"Can you show me other tricks like that?"

"Maybe when you're older."

Fifteen minutes later, they walk through the turnstiles near the paddock of the racetrack when the smell of manure and hay hits Junior in the face. Horses nicker in their stalls while light-weight foam saddles are adjusted. He wins $37 that afternoon. His ideas about money and his father forever changed that day.

Ten years later, Nick's father is sentenced to three years after being caught in a police net while running a long con game. Before leaving his wife and son, he tells Nicky he's the man of the house now, as his mom had become too ill to work anymore. He tells Nicky to use the knowledge he'd imparted to him to separate people from their money by using his home computer to pull off lottery scams, relationship scams (they can be quite fun and titillating at times), and by posing as a potential buyer of a condo or property in another state or country. He knew how to make authentic-looking documents such as cashier's checks complete with watermarks and how to build websites that look official and realistic enough to convince gullible or lonely people that they were lotto winners in other countries or that a fictitious character of his was interested in dating his marks if they would send him money for plane fare. Ninety-five percent of the time, the marks decided not to go through with it, but it only took one sucker to make his monthly income sizable. Hell, it sure beat selling crap products door-to-door or manual labor for minimum wage, and it gave him the ability to make the monthly payments on their house and provide for his mother.

Nicky also developed his own social network of confidence men and women he'd interacted with, initially through contacts with his old man. He dabbled in occasional long schemes with a few of these contacts, but their plans eventually fell through for various reasons.

The day Nicky was pinched, six cops surrounded his apartment building. Two entered via the bedroom door, two through the kitchen, while the other two guarded the front and back doors. Before he could get out of bed, they had his hands zip-cuffed behind his back. They charged him with conspiracy to obtain property by trick or deception and arrested him. They seized his computer and boxes of illicit material in the other bedroom.

He had two other similar arrests, but this time, the cops offered him a deal. Become an undercover informant or do ten years. Help them obtain damning information on others in exchange for a new lease on freedom. He'd been doing so for five years now. Now that his fortieth birthday approached, Nicky sat down with Detective Jameson and handed over the latest dirt on a well-known city politician named Bob.

Jameson wore his black hair slicked back and liked blue suits. "This looks promising, but it's not enough proof, Nick. I need you to set up a meeting with the guy and wear a wire. Same procedure as the others."

Nicky crushed his cigarette butt in the ashtray. "I'm meeting with him in two hours. I want this to be my last job. I've helped you put criminals and pervs behind bars. I've more than earned my freedom from you." He waves his hand around the grungy police station. "From this."

Jameson's brow raises, and a smirk forms on his mouth. "You're in no position to call the shots. I could send you back to prison any time."

"I need to know when this ends. I've played ball with you. I'll wear the wire on this one, but that's it. Cut me loose after Bob. My fortieth is next week. I've given you five years of my life. If I'd done my time, I'd be up for release now with good behavior."

Jameson stands and refills his coffee mug before he walks around the table to where they're sitting. He does three slow revolutions before sitting down again. "Tell you what, *if* you help us nail this pedophile with the goods and *if* you find me, someone, to replace you, I will consider letting you go."

Nicky breathes a sigh of relief, but a thought hits him square in the face. "Does that mean you used someone like me to catch me?"

The smirk again. "You're a smart guy, Nick. Figure it out."

Anger grabs hold of him. Did one of his associates in a long con rat him out? He does his best to compartmentalize the anger. He's felt like a slave for years and wants his life back, whatever the cost. "Wire me up. We do this tonight. Bob invited me to his house in the suburbs. I get him to say the magic words, and then you nab him."

Nick parks in front of the city employee's house once he's buzzed through the electronic gaits. He thumps his chest and asks the control panel in the truck parked down the street if they heard that. The house is a two-story, Tudor-style with mature trees that line the front yard. A tiny row of million-dollar homes.

Bob opens the door and offers Billy (Nick's alias) scotch in his library.

"I want to thank you for all you've done, Billy."

He swishes the brown liquid into the cut crystal glass. "No need to mention it. It's what friends with common interests do for one another."

Bob smiles and puts down his cigar. "Follow me. I want to show you something."

Nick follows him to a part of the mansion he'd never been in, to a marble hallway, and down a flight of steps to a thick, padlocked door of metal and fiberglass. He watches the mark fish a key from his pocket. "Billy, the rooms down here are soundproof, and I can make a video available for you, if you want, my man. You've done so much for me. This is my present to you."

He locks the door behind them, flicks on lights, and leads him to another larger room with cameras in the ceiling. The final light switches on and illuminates a bed. On it is a crescent-shaped bulge. The bulge quickly backs against the far wall the instant light fills the room and metal rattles.

Bob pulls away the blanket to reveal a shaking young girl chained to the wall. She's naked and tears streak down both cheeks. Her eyes fix on the far corner of the room, making sure she doesn't look at her captor.

Nick says, "Why is this girl in chains, Bob?"

Bob reaches for her hair and moves a bang away from her face. "Isn't she magnificent? Thirteen years old but she could pass for seventeen. Look at the hips, the pert breasts, the full pouty lips."

Nick hopes the cops are breaking down the door. "You've converted the basement into a fuck dungeon? Sweet! Where did you get her?"

"Found her downtown, homeless and hungry. I fed her and offered her a place to stay. One thing turned into another, and voila! She's yours to do as you please. I assume you want your time with her captured-on video?"

"Is there a bathroom I can use first?"

Bob points behind them to a door near the entrance. "Be my guest."

Nick pulls out his cell phone once he closes the door to the john, but there's no signal. He wonders what the cops in the van have heard. Nothing Bob said upstairs would trigger them to raid the place. What the hell is he going to do?

He returns from the bathroom to find Bob has manacled the girl's free arm to a bolt in the wall and secured her ankles in leather straps, ones as psych units use. He slaps her across the face after she spits on him. He places duct tape over her mouth and says, "Behave, or I'll use the cattle prod again!"

He turns to Nick and says, "This little whore likes it rough. If you prefer, I can drug her, and you can fuck her mouth, or we can flip her over once the drugs take hold for anal. Or all three.

"I can hit the record button on my way out if you like."

"How do you keep this hidden from your family?"

"Easy. It's soundproofed, and I have the only key. The wife and kids think it's my work office, and they think my work is boring." He knits his brow and says, "Is everything okay with you?"

He needs to stay in character, so he points to the bedbound teen. "She really is hot! This is a great set-up you have. Is she the first one you've had down here?"

Bob frowns. "I fail to see why—"

He doesn't want to blow his cover, so he walks to the bed to fondle and tweak a breast while the girl writhes and struggles against her restraints. It is a feeling of immense, raw power to hold complete control over another person. His hand lingers as she writhes beneath him while he thinks about how to get out of this predicament.

Her movement excites him, and he feels the urge to give in, drop his trousers, and climb onto her. He starts to play with himself through his pants with his other hand. His erection is noticeable through his pants. He says to Bob, "Oh yeah! Before I take you up on your kind offer, I want to video this on my cell phone, but I left it in my car." He says, "I will be right back."

Bob's brow furrows deeply as he thinks. "You've been recorded on tape fondling her. Okay, let's do this."

His breathing is shallow, and his words are clipped. "I love the way she struggles. I think I'll fuck her first, then maybe you can give her the drug. She does have a sweet-looking mouth."

Bob locks the door to the basement behind them, and Nick [Billy] hurries to his car. He acts as if he can't find the phone, but he talks rapidly into his microphone. "He's got a minor chained to a bed downstairs. The door is thick metal, so you won't be able to break it. His present to me is to let me fuck her. You need to follow me inside NOW and take him down!" He still wrestles with his situation and says, "If I don't do this, my cover is blown! Stop me! Free the girl! Arrest him!"

Bob calls to him from the front door. "C'mon, Billy!"

He holds up the phone. "Sorry, it was wedged between the seats."

He sneaks a glance down the street at the van, where there is still no sign of movement. At the front door, he asks, "Where's your family tonight?"

Bob snickers. "The wife took the kids to see her parents. They won't be back until Sunday night."

He lets Bob enter first and acts as if he's closing the front door behind them but leaves it ajar.

Down the steps they go, and Bob unlocks the basement door. He pauses long enough to say, "Damn, I forgot to arm the security system." He walks to the nearby wall and sets it. Immediately, the alarm screeches like a banshee and he looks at the panel, which indicates the front door has been opened. "You closed the door, right?"

Terrified, Nick [Billy] nods as he strains to hear movement upstairs, but there's nothing. "I thought I did."

Bob hurries up the stairs while Nick dials 911 for more cops and an ambulance before he enters the dungeon.

Then, multiple voices filter down from above. He hurries to the shackled girl, places a blanket over her naked body, and says, "I'm working undercover for the cops. You're going to be free soon. The cops are here, and they will arrest the man who kidnapped you. We'll have you out of those chains once we find the keys. I'm Nick, what's your name?"

The girl is in shock and doesn't respond. She trembles, and her breathing is shallow. Her wrists and ankles have deep ligature marks. Her face has several fading yellow bruises, along with fresh ones.

Detective Jameson comes from the van, brings the keys, and frees the girl. A female cop joins him and says, "An ambulance just arrived. They're going to come down with a stretcher and take you to a hospital." After a few cursory questions go unanswered, the lady cop smiles and says, "That's okay. We will talk later after the doctor examines you."

Weeks later, Nick learns the girl is named Tina, and she thinks she was held in the basement for at least a week but can't be sure. After he abducted her, Bob threw away her clothes, starved her, at times drugged her, and made her life a living hell. All of which Bob recorded for posterity. The video evidence seized from the home also shows tapes of three other young girls, whose whereabouts remain a mystery. Bob denies knowing them and making the tapes. Before tonight, Bob was the only male on the impounded videos. Nick was questioned at length about the section of tape that showed him fondling Tina, but the cops agreed he acted so as not to blow his cover. Bob is charged with kidnapping and rape of a minor and is being held without bond. He pleads innocent. Tina is being housed in a local girls' home and is receiving therapy for drug abuse, depression, and PTSD while they search for her mother.

Nick earns his promise of freedom once he agrees to testify if needed and provides Jameson with a potential replacement con artist to take his place.

A Hopeless Place

"If I ever see that woman again, I will snap her neck like a butterbean."

Ray

After a restless sleep, Alicia wakes early, places a call in the morning, and drives two hours to another state in her SUV. During the drive, she experiences double vision and a stabbing headache behind her eyes. She pulls over twice for it to pass. The last stop is at a bar for a Bloody Mary. She buys a second for the road and minutes later reaches her destination. She gets behind a line of predominantly black women and children huddled together and bundled in sweatshirts and jackets. A smattering of whites and Hispanics dot the line in front of and behind her.

She passes through a metal detector and enters a large open waiting area where a female guard pats her down. She waits thirty minutes until another guard instructs her to follow him. She sits at a small table, and a tall, muscular man with a goatee walks in and takes the seat across from her. Six male guards supervise the cluster of tables. The sides of his head are shaved, and the top sports a black crew cut. A tattoo of three interlocking triangles adorns the right forearm, while the left shows a swastika with the words "white power" below it. His workhouse shirt fits tight across his chest.

The last time she saw Ray, he was nineteen, and she was fifteen. He was a good half-brother, protecting her from bullies and her stepfather. When he was a kid, he wanted to be a cop, and Alicia can't remember exactly when that dream went far off the rails.

She makes an effort to smile despite the Nazi symbol. "I like your jailhouse art. How are you doing, Ray?"

He looks her up and down before he grimaces and says, "Why the fuck are you here, sis?"

She casts sideways glances at the guards. "I want to ask you something."

"Speak softly, and don't mention names. There are bugs, and they eavesdrop on family conversations."

She rolls her eyes. "I know how these places operate."

That brings a light smile to his hardened face. "You do, huh? I'd like to hear about it sometime."

She shifts her weight. "I heard from her why you're here. I want to know if it's true."

He closes his eyes and takes a deep breath. A vein pumps away in his temple while he grits his teeth. "Let me tell you about this place. The walls in the living areas have black mold, the ceiling leaks when it rains, there are rats the size of cats, half the showers are non-functioning, there is no warm water, and half the time the heat and air don't work."

She smirks. "Sounds like home life when we were little, thanks to you-know-who."

He looks amazed and scowls. "You still have anything to do with her?"

"I wouldn't, but she enjoys her petty extortions. So, are you here because you got greedy and got pinched after the mark figured out he was a sucker?"

The vein pulses again. "That's what she said?" He laughs. "Her stupid planning tipped off the cops. She drove off and left me to run from the scene on foot; then she had the stones to rat me out to save herself. Told me she'd make it up to me after I did my time. Said she was too old to do more time."

"I thought your ninety days were up. When do you get out?"

"Not any time soon. I stabbed a dude in here who stole from me. He may or may not survive. So, it looks like I will leave this workhouse for a real prison.

"You mentioned the *E*-word. If she's forcing you to work with her, stop it now, any way you can, before you end up here or worse. She was a useless grifter when I knew her, so I can't imagine she's any better now. Get her out of your life."

"How did you get started in the game?"

"You never knew my old man." He laughs. "Lucky for you. He never did an honest day's work in his life and came from a line of counterfeiters, but he never had the knowledge or ability for that, so he ran numbers and did short, small cons on the street. One day, he didn't come home, and we never heard from him again. Jean assumed he'd run off with another woman, but I think he conned the wrong guy out of money, and he's probably in a landfill."

Alicia grunts. "That shines a little light on why I'm the way I am."

Ray's eyes shift to the far side of the meeting area. "What do you mean by that?"

She shakes her head. "Not the time or the place …"

In a far corner of the large area, a fight breaks out between a male prisoner and a woman visitor. Chairs are upended. Both spew curses at the other while he puts his hands around her wide neck, and she tries to knee him in the groin. The guards break it up, but visitation time is cut short for the group. More fights nearly break out because of this decision; visitors are upset that they've driven so far to only have a few minutes. On her way out, Alicia tells herself life isn't fair, so why should the workhouse be? Her worst suspicions about Jean are confirmed. She must initiate her backup plan.

First was Jean, then Ray, then her. It doesn't take a genius to realize who's next.

During the next week, she receives a collect call from Ray in the workhouse. The inmate he stabbed died. He's being transferred tomorrow morning to a prison nine hours away. What began as a ninety-day workhouse stay based on his inability to pay fines and court costs after his arrest as a con man morphed into second-degree murder with a possible fifteen-years-to-life sentence. He may never be a free man again.

She wonders how many others have been in the same boat … sent to the workhouse to work off a court debt only to defend themselves and get charged with a more serious crime.

"That's shit luck, Ray. I wish I could see you again, but there's too much crap going on here with Jean."

"Don't worry about me. Get free of that bitch before she drags you down. Any way you can."

The Storm Before the Storm

"The biggest danger is having a partner who's not who you think they are."

Alicia

When the banks open in the morning, Alicia takes her phony ID to the banks, where Susan Smith opens new accounts and withdraws a total of fifteen grand. She tells the bank teller she's buying a used car with the money, and the transaction occurs without a hitch. Back home, she removes the red-headed wig and celebrates with pizza and a six-pack while she sits back in her recliner to watch four hours of Shark Week she recorded the night before. Two episodes about great white sharks are new this year, and she enjoys seeing new footage of the largest great whites known to man. The largest are all female and they dwarf the divers and photographers that swim near them. The females have multiple large scars along their flanks, and several have them near their snouts. The scars come from mating when the male bites the female to grab onto her and roll her over. In one episode, regular-sized sharks of various kinds are feeding on a whale carcass but suddenly vacate the area minutes before an immense female great white rises from the deep to feed.

"Nice to know they observe a pecking order," Alicia says to herself, smiling. She feels like a great white tonight. After four shows are completed, she tapes the remainder of that night's shark week and drives to *The Corner Bar*. The blurred vision and strong headache behind her eyes return, so she swallows aspirin after she parks.

Nick leans on the bar, smiling and chatting with a young woman dressed in a tank top and tight jeans. Her DDs stretch the black-top to the max, and her ass looks tight enough to bounce a quarter off it. Nick rests his hand on the young woman's arm in a familiar kind of way. Alicia sits down at the other end of the bar and watches her press a piece of paper into his palm. It looks like he may be about to kiss her when the old barfly next to Alicia orders another beer. Nick rises and sees Alicia. He pauses for an instant before retrieving a draft for the barfly. He greets her with a smile and says, "Hey, the usual?"

She stares at him. She's never been exclusive with anyone in her life, but a sudden wave of jealousy washes over her, and she hates the feeling. "Why the hell not?" Her neck suddenly stiffens, and a flood of nausea overcomes her. "Make it a double."

Before he finishes making her martini, the woman with the come-on-me teats calls for him to return to her side of the bar.

Nick puts Alicia's drink on a coaster and says, "You do realize I live off the tips I make?"

She laughs in his face. Gary's stolen check for eight grand cleared, along with many others. "Bullshit, I just took home fifteen bricks, and you did better than me this week, so don't blow smoke up my ass."

He must remain in character as others at the bar can hear them. He hopes the older customers within earshot don't know the slang meaning of the word. He doesn't want to bring more attention to them. He acts like he's wiping the bar down near her and whispers, "Please keep your voice down."

She downs the drink in one long gulp and slides the martini glass his way. "See you after you close tonight. Try to keep your paws off those store-bought teats."

She rises without paying and, at the exit, leaves with another woman—shorter and wearing a heavy winter coat—in tow. They talk briefly in the parking lot until Alicia hands her something, and they go their separate ways.

Alicia pounds the steering wheel with her hands and screams until she thinks it's out of her system. She almost blacks out while her vision blurs. She takes deep breaths and closes her eyes. It feels like the top of her head is about to explode.

When she meets him at his apartment door, it's like nothing's changed with Nick. No mention of the young barfly with the big knockers. It's a struggle to look him in the eye and not stab him with the switchblade she placed in her coat pocket after what she's learned. He makes her a martini while he drinks beer.

The sex is raw and more frenzied than normal; she draws blood on his back and mouth. While he enters her from behind, she cries silent tears. The headache is now always present; it's a sharp, stabbing pain behind and above her eyes. Double vision and neck stiffness return with a vengeance.

Afterward, they share a joint, which helps the pain recede. She kisses him one final time. "Do you have anything you want to share with me?"

His brow furrows while he looks into her eyes for a clue. He laughs and shrugs. "Not that I know of."

"You sure?"

He emits brief nervous laughter and looks about the room. "Yes, I'm sure. What's this about?"

"Nothing. I have a job for us, big pay potential, with another partner of mine," she says.

He puts on his pants and says, "I'm all ears."

Once Alicia describes the game and answers his questions, he says, "It could work; I'm in."

They walk to *Smilin' Sally's,* where a new heavy-set waitress with a short bob haircut takes their food and drink orders. She's efficient, and Alicia is home before two a.m.

She removes all the remaining watches, jewelry, guns, and other stolen items from beneath the living room floorboards and sells them the next day at the two local pawn shops, ignoring her rule about not selling close to home. For this con, she will need all her money and guile to tempt the marks.

❀   ❀   ❀

Nick convinces Alicia to let everyone be targets for the next scam, including her friend Samantha. He plans to play Steve Benson, 34, who's looking to settle down. Nick creates fake personal information and credit cards with Benson's name on it to pay for and set up his dating profile on the most popular dating site in the country.

She helps him create his profile, which starts out saying, "I'm a healthy, strong man of faith who's never been married, with good, old-fashioned Midwestern values who's looking for the love of his life to marry. I'm a people person whose parents raised my sister and me in a warm, loving home. I am a college graduate who works as a motivational instructor. I like baseball and football. I enjoy fishing, camping, line dancing, and karaoke. I'm looking to find a

117

good woman with a beautiful soul—with a strong Christian faith that stresses the importance of family, children, and Jesus Christ—with similar interests who wants to have children. I'd like to share texts and pictures first to get to know you before there's any talk of meeting."

What the unsuspecting targets do not know yet is that "Steve" will claim to be a US Army sergeant stationed in Frankfurt, Germany. Nick buys an authentic-looking Army uniform and camouflage clothes from Military Uniform Supply.

Alicia buzzes his long locks into a short crew cut and then takes pictures of him in uniform, running and doing pull-ups bare-chested. Nick photoshops himself in pictures of the military base in Frankfurt, in town during Oktoberfest, and lastly, going to a local church service.

"Take all the possible pics you think we will ever need because I'm not cutting off my hair again."

"Okay, when I post a profile, I plan to claim to be attracted to elderly men looking for a young wife. There are lots of horny, single geezers out there willing to spend money to chase their pipe dream."

Nick rubs his short hair and sees himself in the mirror. "I figured you'd fight me on this, so I created personal information and a credit card for you and your friend." He hands her several cards. "After my pics are done, you ladies get several outfits together, and I'll take all the photos you want. If you want me to photoshop you in pictures or places, let me know."

She kisses the top of his head and produces a pair of handcuffs. "Let's finish your photos, Sergeant. Then I'll be the drunk slut making a scene in a bar, and you can be the arresting MP who enters and punishes me however you see fit."

He smiles. "You gonna get violent?"

"Of course. Gotta keep you on your toes, and it makes the punishment more fun."

Hours later, after a shower and food, they work on Alicia's profile. Gina Frye, 36, says, "I'm a very giving woman, married and divorced once, no children, willing to relocate in or out of the country who's looking to connect with an older man (45 on up is fine) for an exclusive relationship as men my age run around and are far too immature for me. I'm a homebody who loves to cook, bake, and decorate, but I also enjoy traveling, nice restaurants, and dressing up to attend parties or sports events. Let's learn more about each other via texts and share pictures."

The next day, Alicia and her friend Samantha arrive with all sorts of clothes, lingerie, make-up, push-up bras, and bathing suits to wear for their photo shoots. Samantha chooses to be Eva Jones, 29, who works as an executive for a high-end women's clothier. She brings her own narrative, which passes muster with Nick and Alicia. It takes longer than expected to find the right set of looks for the women— shy but available, girl-next-door, come-hither, and in others, a tad slutty to downright raunchy. Nick marvels at the wonders of the push-up bra, which causes a diversion from the shoot for all three until the next morning. Later that night, they choose the initial sets of pictures to share they hope will attract the greatest number of responses (Nick downloads ones with him exercising shirtless and a handsome headshot, Alicia downloads a girl-next-door shot with a come-hither look, while Samantha poses as the fashion-conscious businesswoman) then they complete the mundane series of questions required by the dating sight. Everything meets with company approval, and their dating sites are officially open.

Alicia receives the first response, followed by Samantha. Most of the men want to meet them now and share their numbers with Alicia and Samantha. They turn them down politely but remain intrigued by their high-end lifestyles and lead them on with their replies. They ask what their interests are and await their responses.

Nick receives a wave of replies, all commenting on his six-pack body and handsome face. Almost every one of them goes into detail about what is important to them and their value systems. Most say they're interested in marriage, but a few say no marriage. They ask where he lives and what exactly a motivational instructor does. Together the three scammers write replies to every respondent and request they all provide their personal e-mail so their correspondence can continue free of the website. So far, the female respondents are more adept at following the instructions of the wannabe scammers.

Some targets don't respond, but most provide their e-mail addresses. Many send pictures of themselves. Nick cringes at most of the photos of the women his post attracted. He would never date them due to age, looks, and/or weight. Their stories are mostly filled with heartbreak, divorce, and hints of past abuse, but they claim now to be born-again Christians. Precious few look doable or hot, and I want to hook up with him now.

The first pictures from the male respondents contain numerous dirty photos and some facial shots. Alicia smirks at the percentage of men that think a picture of their penis will cause women to swoon. Several men claim to own boats, and one guy flies his own plane. The women choose separate responses designed to play on what they perceive as each man's weakness.

All three return their own responses until they feel comfortable asking for money from their marks. Nick reveals to his respondents that he's in the US Army stationed in Germany and shares the photoshopped pictures. Alicia and Samantha send more suggestive photos and language to their most rabid responders.

While they build desperation in their future marks, the trio scout smaller jewelry and clothing stores to develop a list of potential targets for gypsy scams and make notes of staff patterns and the locations of video cameras. On their first attempt at a jewelry store, Alicia and Nick pose as a couple interested in a ring, and while they command the full attention of a young salesclerk and block the clerk's view of Samantha, she reaches over the counter and boosts several sets of earrings and bracelets. She tugs on Alicia's coat as the signal, and Alicia abruptly changes her mind about the purchase. Once out of the store, they hurry to Alicia's SUV and drive to a mall. At a clothing store, they wait for an employee to go on lunch break before they ask the remaining staffer to check in the back for a pair of jeans in a certain size. Once the employee does so, Nick hops the counter, opens the register, and scoops up the cash. Before the employee returns to let them know she doesn't have the size, Nick hops back in front of the counter. They thank her and leave.

They eat lunch with some of the money from the register and plan for the next day. They divide the rest of their loot, and Nick drops the women off at Alicia's. Things are going so well Nick doesn't call Jameson. He's eager to see what the relationship scams bring and takes a nap before it's time for his shift at the bar.

A Room with No View

"If you do this job long enough, you develop a hard outer shell, or the heartache and sadness will devour you."

Miss Givens

On her drive home, Alicia sees a young woman on the street walking her daughter on a harness leash.

A minute later, her breathing becomes shallow; she clutches her throat and pulls over in the break-down lane. She rolls down the window and gulps for air. She thinks she must be having a heart attack or is dying from that damn aneurysm.

She closes her eyes for a long time until something strange happens. She sees herself back in that musty, cold basement of her childhood.

She imagines herself leaving the house as a six-year-old and walking to the next-door neighbor in search of her mother. Mrs. Newton is a widow and lets her sit at the kitchen table, have milk and cookies, and later watch cartoons. Hours later, they see her mother walk down the sidewalk and go to meet her.

Mrs. Newton wraps her sweater around herself. She smells perfume and possibly alcohol on Jean's breath. "Jean, your little one came over to my house looking for you."

"She knows better than that. I told her I had to run to the store for a few things."

"She's awfully young to be left alone. Where are your groceries?'

"I only left her for a few minutes, and the items are in my purse. Sorry to bother you." Jean tugs on Alicia's arm.

"Jean, she's been in my kitchen waiting for three hours."

She looks at her watch. "You're mistaken. It's been fifteen minutes." Then, to Alicia: I bought you candy. Let's get home.

Mrs. Newton watches Jean stagger home with Alicia in tow. "You're welcome," she calls out.

In the next memory, her ankle is attached to a metal chain attached to the floor near the drainpipe and she's been alone in the house for two days. Dried tears streak her face, and she worries that her mother may never return. What if something happens to her—if she is hurt or steps in front of a bus or is hospitalized or just plain leaves her—who will come and save her? Who will take care of her? The chain was a recent addition after the Mrs. Newton incident. She was locked in the basement while her mother searched for the next man in her life at local bars. She'd eaten the last sandwich mother left for her yesterday, even after a cockroach crawled on it. Today, she accidentally spilled the last of her water on the floor. She relieved herself over the drainpipe, curled into a ball on the mattress, and tried to sleep. On the third day, Mother came home and was not alone. She cried out for her to come down and release her; her throat was dry and she'd defecated on the mattress, but the stereo on the main floor drowned out her screams. The next morning, mother came down and released her after hours of noise coming from the main floor. When Jean spotted the soiled mattress, she beat her with a broom handle and ran a bath.

"I'm trying to improve our lives, and this is how you repay my efforts?" she yells at Alicia. "Do you want to live like this? I know I don't."

She apologizes over and over until the tears flow again.

Weeks later, a woman knocks on the door while Alicia is at school.

"I'm Miss Givens from Family Services. May I come in?"

Jean reluctantly opens the door and invites her into the kitchen.

"We received a complaint that you left your young daughter Alicia, aged six, alone at home for extended periods of time."

She folds her arms across her chest and laughs. "Did old lady Newton next door tell you this? You know she's senile, and she doesn't like me."

"This is no laughing matter, I assure you, and this isn't the only complaint we've received from you, either."

Mrs. Newton spends the next hour interviewing her and taking a tour of the home.

Thus began the decade of DFS involvement and temporary emergency placements in foster homes while Jean made attempts to clean up herself and the house. Alicia was sexually and physically abused in several of them. She ran away numerous times, and no family adopted her permanently, so DFS reluctantly returned to her mother.

Heart Breakers

"Life itself is a brief scam. We all wear masks and hide who we really are from the world. No one knows the real me and that's how I like it."

Alicia

Alicia pawns the jewelry and hands Nick his share of the take after she grabs a seat at the bar. He brings her a Grey Goose martini while she gives the stink eye to the same young woman in a different tube top at the other end of the bar.

Near closing time, Nick approaches Alicia with another martini. "I think it's time for the good sergeant to take his groupies to the final level."

"What's the angle?"

"That the good sergeant goes on leave soon and wants to meet them but doesn't have money for the plane ticket. That he will pay them back next month when his paycheck arrives."

She sips and nods. "Okay. All we need is one or two. I think we've all primed the pump. How about we meet at your place tomorrow at 2 pm?"

Tube Top calls to Nick for a refill. She waves her empty beer glass his way and turns her head to smile at Alicia with velvet menace.

Her head pounds, and the double vision returns. "I may rip out that skank's hair by the roots," Alicia says, loud enough to carry across the bar.

"I hope you don't," Nick whispers. "I plan to buy this place one day, and I need every customer and more."

"This shit hole? You can buy a better one that has good bar food and classier customers. A place that doesn't cater to whores in tube tops and leather skirts. I've heard that Barfly sells blow jobs in the parking lot after closing."

Nick announces, "Last call!" Then, softly to Alicia, he says, "That's a victimless crime." He refills the tube top's glass, and she flirts with him while she grins at Alicia.

Alicia gives her the finger, then admits to herself Nick should get a finger as well.

Back at his place, Alicia paces. "If she's not a whore, what is she?"

Nick changes his shirt, which smells of smoke and fast-food oil. "I don't know or care. Jealousy isn't your color, babe. Let it go."

The double-vision and pain behind the eyes return. "Where's the aspirin? My head is splitting."

She runs a bath and covers her face with a wet washrag.

Thirty minutes later, he puts the lid of the toilet down and sits. He inhales deeply and passes her the joint.

"I looked up flights from the Midwest to Frankfurt and the dirt cheapest goes for $1800, so I think we can ask for at least 2K. We open it up to older marks and maybe we could get five suckers to bite."

The rag back on her face, her head turns toward him. "Doubtful. Your personal says you're looking for a woman of child-bearing years to start a family, remember?"

"Maybe some rich older women will gloss over that and want this hunky package you see before you to visit them?"

She throws the rag in his face. "Why would they fall for you when they can call an escort service and pay a fraction of the cost? We'll be lucky if we get one or two bites."

"What are the plans for Sam and you?"

She rises from the tub and grabs a yellow towel to wrap around her body. She sways her hips in a sultry, sexual rhythm. "I'm thinking of responding hot and heavy to the ones farthest away with risqué pictures, the ones who claim to be loaded, offering hot sex in exchange for a getaway vacation to someplace warm with a beach. If they send money for a plane ticket and incidentals like a new beach wardrobe, then we're all yours, baby! A man who responded to Sam mentioned he had access to a private jet. That would be awesome to get close to someone like that!"

Nick laughs as he unwraps Alicia from the towel. "His comment could mean he's a plane mechanic. Remember, every person who responds to our personals is also lying through their teeth to get what they want. Some people will do anything to get what they want."

She steps out of the tub and grins while she lowers her voice. "What is it that you want?"

To be a free man again and get away from trash like you. He smiles, "I think you know."

They don't make it to the bedroom. He positions her on the sink and enters her while she moans and scratches his back. She smears blood from his back to the sides of his face until he looks like an Indian wearing war paint. She comes twice before he manages a weak ejaculation.

It's getting more difficult for him to maintain the ruse the closer he gets to earning his freedom.

Alicia returns to Nick's at 2 pm with her step-sister. "Everyone, this is Missy. She's here to learn how to be a player. She's cool. She's my protégé. She's blood and she wants to be on her own with certain job skills. No 9-to-5 at Mickey D's bullshit for her."

Nick frowns and protests this is not the time to introduce a new, untrusted member, but Alicia shuts him down repeatedly. He finally throws his hands in the air and shakes his head, knowing she'd dig her heels in.

Missy looks sheepish and ready to cry.

They discuss how to handle the marks that responded to their personal ads and Alicia shows Missy how the operation runs. After their meeting, Alicia takes Missy to a nearby subdivision to steal more mail and introduces her to their check-washing scam.

Two weeks later, Nick receives a Western Union wire transfer for $2500 to buy plane tickets to south Alabama, where Lyda Mae Cooper lives in a small farming town. In a personal e-mail, she wrote, "I can hardly wait for your visit. I live in Burnt Corn, Alabama. The money comes from my inheritance, which also includes the family farm after my parents were killed in a car accident. You said you like to fish, and the land has a pond with bluegill, bass, and catfish. The settlement money should help make us comfortable, along with you working the farm while I raise our family. I added extra money for you to rent a car from the Montgomery airport and for food and gas. I bought a new dress and had my hair done. I am so excited!"

She includes the post office box and directions from the airport. Nineteen words were misspelled in the text.

Alicia receives two cash replies and Samantha three.

Between the three of them, they collected $11,400 from their marks the next day. Alicia brings Missy back to Nick's apartment to finish teaching her the check-washing process.

Midway through the removal of the ink, they hear splintering noises followed by a loud boom and the hurried footsteps of people rushing up the stairs. The crisscross of flashlights floods the room as men roughly pin Nick to the floor and cuff his hands behind his back before he can reach his handgun. Others easily subdue and cuff the women before Alicia can destroy evidence. She unleashes a string of profanities at the cops, and Missy cries when the zip ties pinch her chubby wrists.

One of the cops kicks Alicia, and she responds by tripping him. The cop pulls out his baton, but before he can wield it, she charges him, and they fall to the floor. Though Alicia has her hands behind her back, she climbs on top of him and bites him, drawing blood.

The middle-aged cop screams and rolls them over. He slams her head several times on the hardwood floor until he can wrench his face from her teeth. She stops moving. Missy screams upon seeing Alicia knocked unconscious and continues to wail when two cops escort Samantha to a cruiser. As two others lift the still-screaming Missy and walk her to the door, Alicia's supine body twitches with seizure activity.

Detective Jameson instructs one of the two remaining cops to call for an ambulance while the other makes sure that her airway is clear. Alicia's bladder empties, and she's unresponsive.

"Damn, Ross! What did you do?"

Ross removes the bloody towel from his face and says, "I did what I had to do to get free. She took a big bite out of my face. That woman is crazy strong!"

"Did the other women see this?"

"The young screamer did."

Jameson frowns. "She looks like she could be a minor."

Ross nods his head toward Nick and says, "What about him?"

"I'll bring him downstairs."

The ambulance crew arrives, and Jameson tells them to take her to a hospital immediately.

Jameson tells Ross and his partner, "Follow the ambulance, make sure she's cuffed to the hospital bed at all times, and guard her until you hear from me."

Alone with Nick, Jameson says, "Who are all these fucking women?"

"Untie me, and I'll tell you."

He slices through the plastic knife with a switchblade and says, "I'm listening."

Nick rubs the feeling back into his red wrists. "The woman Ross hurt is Alicia. She was to be my replacement. She never told me, but I think she has serious health problems. You better hope she doesn't die. The other woman about her age may be named Samantha, but I think it's an alias. They've been con partners over the years. The chubby young crier is Alicia's stepsister. She was just here for the first time so that Alicia could teach her con games. She lives with Alicia's mother and has nothing to do with anything. She's a kid, seems kinda slow."

"Stay here while I interview them. I will cuff you later and make sure they see you arrested as well. Hand over what you produced this week. Consider it your final installment."

Nick passes him the money they collected this week.

Jameson returns in fifteen minutes to find Nick doing shots and chewing beef jerky.

He helps himself to the bottle of Jack and grabs a slice of dried beef. "Alicia is on her way to the hospital. Samantha Downs, AKA Terry Bailey, AKA June Cosgrove, is wanted in Italy for human trafficking and solicitation. They want her bad." He takes a healthy pull from the bottle and says, "It might not be your day, Nicky boy."

"Oh, no. Don't do this to me. We had a deal—"

"It's not my fault she became belligerent during the arrest."

"The cop was out of line. I saw what he did—"

"Slow down, ace. You're not in a position to make threats or be a credible witness." Jameson takes the last beef strip from Nick. "We might be able to make this work."

"We?"

Jameson drains the bottle and smiles. "Let me cuff you again and walk you to the car. You want them to know you're also under arrest, don't you?"

❁　❁　❁

Nick has Jameson drop him at the hospital and tells the staff he's Alicia's brother. A cop sits in a chair outside her room. Her wrist is cuffed to the side of the bed, and a large wrap is around her head. He stands there staring at her sleep when a nurse enters.

"Your sister is in and out of consciousness. Her condition is guarded. We await test results to determine how to proceed, and surgery is a possibility, given those head wounds. Hearing a familiar voice may help."

Nick slides a chair over to the bedside after the nurse exits. He holds her hand and says, "I'm sorry you got involved with me. You don't know who, or even what, I am. I've lied to you from day one. I guess you'd call me a snitch for Detective Jameson, though, to me, it seems I'm more like his permanent prisoner. I go undercover for him to help bust perverts and criminals like you. Why? I got caught doing scams, and working with him has been the only way to stay out of jail." He squeezes her hand tighter. "He said if I could find someone to take my place, he'd let me go. I was planning to use you as the ticket to regain my freedom."

He looks at her again and sees her eyes open. In a feeble voice, she asks, "Is that you, Nick?"

He smiles and wonders how much she's understood of his confession. "It's me. The staff says you're going to be alright."

She swallows once and beckons him closer to her mouth. "I wanted to go out on my own terms, but it doesn't look like it's in the cards. If I don't make it, go to my place. There's a key under the potted plant on the stoop and a note on my nightstand. Take care of Jack."

Before he can respond, the nurse and two male orderlies rush into the tiny room that smells of disinfectant. The nurse says, "She needs emergency brain surgery. The doctor will meet with you in the waiting room afterward."

Two hours later, a surgeon in a green gown enters the waiting room. "We were wrapping up the process of relieving the pressure on your sister's brain when her aneurysm burst. She died in a matter of minutes, but she was not in pain."

Nick leaves the room while the doctor is still talking. He takes a crosstown bus to his apartment, opens a new bottle of Jack Daniels, and then remembers about the dog. He drives to Alicia's house. She was in an especially dark mood the night she raised the package to his view before she placed it on his nightstand. She said, "Open this only if I die."

He puts down the bottle and reads what Alicia wrote.

"If you're reading this, it means I'm dead. Likely from a brain aneurysm and hopefully not from something even more violent than that, which is hard to imagine. I also have a rare blood disorder and have already lived longer than my anticipated lifespan. I enjoyed our time together and hope you did too, so I'm asking you to carry out my last wishes since my family won't. I want you to find a good home for Jack. He's not used to anyone but me, so he will be a handful. He does like treats, so good luck with him. If you can't find a home or a good business for him to guard at night, I understand, but please try. I sold my entire stash of cash, guns, and jewelry in the house. There is not much equity in the place, but whatever it sells for, I put your name as the beneficiary. I don't want my mom, Jean, to get a penny of it, and she will try her best to take it from you. She's pure evil. She's been blackmailing me and hung me out to dry during our long con together. I feel bad for Missy, who lives with her, which is why I wanted to show her the ropes of the con game so she doesn't have to depend on a man or Jean to support her.

Bye, Alicia

P.S. This has been bugging me. I know you are way out of my league, so I asked myself why you came on to me in the first place. I've also noticed you follow me home a couple of times, and these two things got me wondering. And there was also something about your demeanor. You seemed to hide a part of yourself from me; I think you're smarter than some bartender who wants to eventually buy a bar. The grifter in me wonders if you're a cop or working with them. If I'm dead and you're reading this, it makes no difference. If your curiosity got the best of you and you opened this while I'm alive, I demand the truth.

P.P.S. If I'm dead, I want you to scatter my ashes in the little pond in Shaw Park. Some of my best early memories were there.

He drinks the rest of the night until he passes out.

In the morning, Jameson leaves a message on his phone. "Meet me at the usual place at noon."

He buys a breakfast burrito and soda. When he arrives at the bench by the lake with the ducks, Jameson is already there, visibly upset he had to wait. No one else is near their section of the park.

Jameson's blue eyes stare hard at him. "You still owe me someone to replace you."

"It was supposed to be Alicia, but your idiot in blue killed her."

"From what I hear, she had an aneurysm ready to blow any day. Her days were numbered. Not his fault, and 'Samantha' is being extradited, so it's either you or the budding criminal."

Nick thinks that could explain part of her odd behaviors. He can't believe what's about to escape his mouth. "Got another idea. The kid doesn't know dick about con games. She's never done one. What about Alicia's mother instead? She worked a con with Alicia recently and has been doing them off and on for decades."

"What dirt do we have on her?"

Nick shrugs. "Alicia said they did a con at a local hotel that had a convention, and they made off with credit cards, cash, and jewelry." He knows who to ask for the details.

"Give me the date and hotel name and Jean's address. I will consider it. If I say no, you're still my guy."

He starts to complain but keeps his mouth shut.

The End of the Line?

"You gotta keep moving in life, or, like a shark, you die. Or so Alicia told me."

Nick

Two months later, Nick receives cash from the sale of Alicia's home and carries her ashes to Clayton Park dawn. Alone, he releases the ashes into the small pond and watches fish rise to nibble the unexpected food.

"This shouldn't have happened, babe. I'm sorry."

He walks to his Camry and drives for a leisurely breakfast in Clayton. At the table, his phone rings, and Jameson tells him, "Today's your lucky day, sport. I have enough dirt on Jean and arrested her today. She's willing to cooperate in exchange for a suspended sentence. So, it looks like you're a free man. Keep your nose clean, or you're back under my thumb."

"You still have her in custody?"

"For about another hour. Wh—"

Nick disconnects the line. He screams yes in the restaurant, prompting curious looks from other customers. He drives to Jean's apartment, and Missy opens the door. He hands her a thick wad of bills. "Alicia wanted me to give you this for you and your brother. It should give you a measure of freedom from Jean. I'm sorry Alicia's dead. Don't let Jean run your life."

Nick drives back to Clayton as he plans to put his offer on the failing bar. Walking along Bonhomme Street, in front of the Sevens Building, he bumps into a man who's not looking where he's walking. The man is of indeterminate age; he may be forty years old or more, and he's of average height and weight. They apologize to each other. Nick is hit by an overwhelming sense of fear at his touch and has a fleeting thought that this man is somehow a predator, not unlike Alicia's morbid fascination with deadly sharks. He hurries to put distance between them, but they both enter the Sevens Building. The stranger waits for an elevator while Nick enters the nearest bathroom to throw water on his face and catch his breath. Slowly, his blood pressure returns to normal, and the feeling of discombobulation abates.

The rest of the day, he can't shake the impact of bumping into the stranger until his happiness over his newfound freedom from Detective Jameson takes over. He puts a lowball offer on the bar and tosses a penny into the nearest fountain. He buys a bottle of Woodford Reserve and a track program to celebrate, not stopping twice to think the price of his freedom means that someone like Jean must take his place.

If they accept his offer to buy the bar, it means his life is certainly turning around for the better. After a winning day at the track, he calls Gretchen, the busty barfly in the tube top, and invites her to his place to celebrate. He feels like a new man.

Life is good. If a con man can reinvent himself by swimming to new waters, so much the better.

The End

Acknowledgments

Part of this story happened to me when I was married. Some close friends will understand because I shared it with them years ago, but I will not recount that here out of respect for certain people and my own sanity. Many of the specifics happened exactly as I've laid them out (from my memory), scattered throughout all the fictitious sections. If I told them to you, you'd be shocked or may not believe me, but I've been called worse than a liar. Some crazy real-life situations happen to us all in time, but the story about the con artists I laid out is all fiction. This is a work of fiction set in an unnamed fictional town near St. Louis with fictional establishments.

I set out to write this story replete with unsavory characters and found out along the way I needed (for my own sanity) one sympathetic character, so I tried to make the most disturbed person relatable on some level. Some may agree I succeeded; others may not. That's fine. It's a story I made up, after all.

My initial plan was to write two novellas (*Mating Scars* and *Death Rattles*) and lump them into one book, but my publisher suggested publishing *Mating Scars* first. It made sense since I have yet to complete *Death Rattles*. For my faithful readers who read all my work, I want you to know that a character at the end of *Mating Scars* makes an early appearance in *Deah Rattles*.

My sincere thanks once again go out to New York Book Publishers, specifically Lisa "Tokyo" Smith, Connor Stewart, editor James Stewart, Logan Walsh, Jessica Cohen, Emma Becker, and Jeremiah Hofsted. Plus, everyone else who worked on *Mating Scars* to get it formatted and ready for print and those who continue to hone my website: scottlmillerbooks.com.

I hope you enjoyed my strange little tale. One way to thank an author is to leave a review. It doesn't have to be lengthy, but positive reviews are appreciated. You may do so on my website, Amazon, or other sites.